Pepped Up

Ali Dean

Editor: Leanne Rabesa

http://editingjuggernaut.wordpress.com/

Cover: Sarah Foster

http://sprinklesontopstudios.com/

Chapter 1

This right here is what I live for. The steady rhythm of my feet landing softly on dirt. Colorado sunshine heating the fresh morning air. Birds singing as they swoop in and out of trees. And Dave frolicking beside me with his tongue lolling out to the side.

I want to capture the exhilaration and peace flowing through my veins, pulsing through my soul. Who needs a vice when you can attain an utter sense of being alive with such simple ingredients? Blue sky, fresh air, and, of course, man's best friend. Dave's feeling it, too - runner's high. Endorphin rush. Call it what you will.

We turn off the single track and cross the footbridge separating the foothills from Brockton's residential neighborhoods. I could easily run for another hour or two, but my training schedule calls for a forty-five-minute easy jog, and I'm already pushing an hour.

I used to think that being a disciplined athlete was all about pushing hard. But I was wrong. It's really about knowing when to hold back, being patient enough to do it, and then pushing hard when the time comes.

I got into running on my first day of high school, almost by accident. Having never played sports when I was younger, I was pretty clueless about how they worked, but it turned out I was fast – *really* fast – and immediately made varsity and even qualified for the State meet. But since I had no idea of strategy, starting every run with a full-on sprint was all I knew to do, so "crash and burn" became my motto for the first few races.

I now have two cross country seasons and two track seasons under my belt, and I've learned how to pace myself at races and in workouts. But this season presents a new challenge. I need to pace myself over the course of the whole season. Not just for twenty minutes or so, but for three and a half months, or fourteen weeks.

I'm usually beat, mentally and physically, after the State meet, but if all goes well, I'll be racing for a month longer than past seasons. First I have to qualify for Regionals at the State meet, and then I have to qualify for Nationals at Regionals. Until then, I've got to hold back. Easier said than done.

I wind through the familiar streets, my empty stomach coming to attention when the smell of bacon from someone's kitchen floats by. When I turn onto Shadow Lane, slowing to a walk for my cool-down, I see a silver Mercedes Benz pulling up in front of the Wilders' house. I narrow my eyes at it, watching Jace Wilder get out from the passenger side. His biceps flex as he holds the top of the door to lean in the open window and say something to the driver. Reaching in the car window, he retrieves a box of donuts before walking towards his house.

The car drives away from the Wilders' house in my direction and slows as it passes me on the sidewalk. I recognize Madeline Brescoll when she rolls down her window. "Hi, Pepper." Her voice is filled with self-satisfaction. Through the window, I can see she looks gorgeous as usual.

I raise my hand in an unenthusiastic wave. "Morning."

She flashes me an insincere smile, turns up the radio and drives away. I glance down at Dave, who's licking sweat off my shin. He's unimpressed. He might be the first male of any species to snub her like that.

Dave's a multi-colored, short-haired mutt I adopted pretty much by accident last year – I simply wasn't capable of ignoring the "free puppies" sign. Clearly, despite his lack of pedigree, he's far too good for the Madeline Brescolls of this world.

Madeline's family owns one of the largest breweries in the nation. She goes to Lincoln Academy, the private school in town. And along with the rest of the female population in Brockton, she wants Jace Wilder.

Admittedly, Madeline has actually succeeded to some degree in her efforts to get him. Jace sleeps with her more regularly than any other girl and, according to the gossip, she's the only girl he's been with in his grade. Apparently Jace only hooks up with older girls these days; I imagine that will change now that he's a senior, unless he moves on to college girls.

I shake off my thoughts as I stretch my hamstrings. I'm determined not to let boys, or one boy in particular, ruin the buzz from my morning run. High school drama isn't something I've let invade my life in the past two years, and junior year won't be any different.

It doesn't matter to me who our class officers are, or who won Homecoming Queen - my life revolves around running, and all my friends are runners except for Jace. It's the one thing I have where I can stand out. I'm not an amazing student. I'm not popular. I'm not in band, on debate team, or dating anyone, let alone the starting quarterback (that would be Jace, by the way). Running is my thing. And this season is going to be epic.

I jog up the stairs to the second-floor apartment I share with my Gran. She's singing along to Aretha in her bedroom, meaning she'll be out soon and looking for her coffee, so I hit the kitchen before the bathroom. I don't drink the stuff myself, but Gran's an addict and I know she'll want some any minute.

Ten minutes later I'm out of the shower and tugging a brush through my wet hair when I hear the unmistakable sound of Jace's voice in the kitchen with Gran. I quickly clasp my favorite purple bra behind my back and pull on a pair of red cutoff jean shorts from my closet floor. I'm pushing my arms through the holes of a snug grey tee shirt when I hear Gran in the doorway to my bedroom.

"Nice bra, Pep. You got matching undies?" She grins and wiggles her eyebrows.

"I'm going commando today, Gran," I tease.

"Not in those short little shorts you ain't. I can practically see your butt cheeks hangin' out." She waves her index finger in mock disapproval. "Not that you got much in the way of butt cheeks, but if you did, they'd be hangin' out of those little scraps of fabric."

I make a face in response. "Whatever, Gran, I have to race for twenty minutes in front of hundreds of people in a uniform that covers less skin than these, and it's required by the school. And I *am* wearing underwear." I pull down the shorts a bit and pull up my polka-dotted panties. "But they don't match the bra. Sorry to disappoint."

"Can I see?" Jace peeks over Gran's shoulder into my bedroom.

"Young man!" Gran elbows him away and we follow her down the hallway. Her piglet slippers oink with each step as she patters towards the kitchen. Gran's looking her usual snazzy self in a butterfly-patterned pajama set, her wiry grey hair sticking out in all directions.

"Happy birthday, old lady." I wrap my arms around her soft little body and rock her back and forth. "Love you, Gran."

She pats me on the back. "I know you do, hun. Now, eat a few donuts. You need some butt cheeks." She pushes a box of a dozen donuts in my direction. "Jace brought over a good selection."

I glance in his direction and raise my eyebrows. He must have stopped at the donut shop with Madeline. After a sleepover at her place, I presume. Jace shrugs and takes a giant bite from a jelly-filled one.

I let my eyes linger a moment. I haven't seen him in a couple of weeks and his olive skin has turned to a dark tan. His jet black hair is ruffled in a messy fauxhawk. He's had the same haircut for long enough that it falls into place without the need for styling.

Jace takes a seat at our dinner table. At six feet three inches, his presence dominates our little apartment even when he's seated.

"Hey, I wasn't gonna miss seeing Buns on her birthday. Got up early just for you." Jace says, winking at Gran.

Gran practically raised Jace, whose mom left when he was four years old. My parents died in a car crash when I was a toddler myself, and Gramps (Gran's hubby) passed shortly after that. Jace's dad, Jim, is a cool guy, but he works full time, so Gran babysat Jace when we were little, and watched us after school as we got older. Gramps was able to leave us a little to live on from his hard work as an electrician over the years, but it was Gran's pension from her days as a U.S. postal mail-woman that allowed her to retire and raise me.

"You're a sweetie," Gran tells Jace. "You could come to the party at Lulu's later. We're having a luncheon," she offers.

I laugh. "You sure that's a good idea, Gran?" Lulu is Gran's BFF. She's throwing a birthday party with all the ladies from Gran's knitting and book clubs. I can just imagine the reaction they'd have to Jace. Teenage girls aren't the only ones affected by his charms.

"Sorry Buns, I can't miss football," he answers, and to his credit he actually sounds regretful.

"So how was the camp?" I ask. He's been in Texas for two weeks playing football. It was for college recruitment and he had to be specially selected to attend.

"It was intense, but a good time. I met some cool guys. We pretty much just played a shitload of football." He mimes throwing a pass. "Slept a ton. Ate a ton. They actually had some decent food at the cafeteria." He glances at Gran and quickly adds, "Nothing like your cooking, Buns, obviously."

Jace feeds the rest of his donut to Dave, who has been waiting patiently with his head resting on Jace's lap.

I shake my head at the resulting crumb-and-drool fest. "So was it worth missing Brockton's preseason? Did they have a lot of recruiters?"

Jace shifts in his seat. "Yeah, they had coaches from all over the nation. But shit, hosting the camp in Dallas in the middle of August pretty much killed any idea that I'd end up anyplace south of Colorado. It's hot as fuck there."

"Yeah, probably not the best recruiting tactic for the southern schools, huh?" I want to ask him if he's considering staying in Colorado, but I'm afraid what his answer will be. I'd like to hold on to the hope that he's not leaving for just a little bit longer. After all, most Brockton Public students go to CU. It's a great school, and in-state tuition is a sweet deal.

"How's your dad doing? I haven't run into him lately," Gran asks.

"Same old. New girlfriend. He's good though. We had dinner at the Tavern last night after I got in. I was hoping to see you there, Pep."

"I had the night off." You could have swung by the apartment to say hello, I want to add. But no, he had to go out and have a sleepover with Madeline. God forbid he goes longer than two weeks without any action. Although, knowing him, he probably figured out a way to meet girls even while he was at football camp.

"Oh hey, I ordered a sick 2000 piece Hendrix puzzle. You want to come over later to start working on it?" Jace asks.

Darn. I wish I could. I really missed him these past two weeks. "I've got my last shift at the Tavern after Gran's party. But don't start it without me. Maybe tomorrow night? We probably won't have much homework after the first day anyway." Not that homework ever got in the way of Jace's social life before.

"Yeah, this one's definitely gonna make the wall, Pep. It's wild." When we were kids, Gran put the best puzzles we finished in frames to hang on the walls. We continue to do it with the really awesome ones.

Jace hangs out for another hour before heading out. "Pick you up at 7:45 tomorrow morning?" he asks me.

"I'll be ready."

I've had my license for a few months but I don't have my own car. When Jace is the one giving me rides, there's not a whole lot of motivation to save up for my own vehicle. It's my time with him. Once we get to school, he does his own thing with his crowd, and I do mine. He usually comes over for dinner, but aside from that, and the occasional puzzle session, driving to school is my special Jace time.

On the one hand, it kind of looks like I'm pining after the guy I can't have, but on the other, he's my oldest friend and I know he cares about me. I know where I stand, and I accept it. Most of the time.

Chapter 2

I was about to start the eighth grade when I realized just how hot Jace was. I guess I always knew that Jace was attractive, because really, girls had crushes on him all the way back to kindergarten. But it wasn't until the last day of the summer before Jace started high school that my general acknowledgment of Jace's hotness turned into acute awareness. And I didn't like it one bit.

I was lying on a beach recliner by Wesley Jamison's pool reading the sixth Harry Potter book. Wes and Jace had just gotten out of the pool and were walking in my direction, threatening to soak me. It'd been a mellow day so far. The boys had had their first day off from football preseason after two weeks of practices. Gran had dropped me and Jace off at Wes's place that morning, and I'd been engrossed in my book and catching some rays for the past hour and a half.

"Better get your book out of the way, Pepper!" Wes called as he charged towards me. I threw my book to the side just as he scooped me up. It wasn't as amazing a feat as it might seem -- at thirteen years old, I probably didn't even hit 100 pounds soaking wet.

"Wesley Jamison!" I pounded my fists on his chest. "Put me down!"

"But you looked like you were getting a little warm in the sun. Don't you want to cool off?" Wes's blue eyes glinted and he grinned at me.

I felt Jace reach around and pluck off my sunglasses just before Wes tossed me in the pool. My arms and legs flailed as I hit the water. "You!" I pointed my finger at Wes while treading water. "And you!" I pointed at Jace.

"Me?" Jace asked, all false innocence. "What did I do?"

I glared at him. "You didn't stop him!" The boys laughed as I swam to the edge to hop out. It did feel good to cool off but now I'd have to be careful not to get my book wet.

They joined me in the recliners, talking about the players on their teams, and joking about how weird it would be to play against each other. Wes would be attending the local private school, Lincoln Academy, and Jace was headed to Brockton Public. They had both made varsity as freshmen, but it was a bigger deal to be on varsity at Brockton. I was pretty sure only one other freshman had made the team.

"Will you guys even play each other? Isn't Lincoln in a different division?" I asked.

"Yeah, it's 4A, not quite big enough to be 5A. I think there's like a thousand kids at Lincoln," Wes replied.

"5A is the sports division for the biggest schools right? And 4A is second biggest?" I asked. I didn't pay much attention to sports, but with all the time I spent with Jace and Wes, it was impossible to remain totally ignorant.

"Yup," Wes confirmed. "I think you need five hundred a class or something to be 5A."

"Brockton's one of the biggest high school's in Colorado," Jace added. "That's why we kick everyone's asses in sports. We've got about 4000 students this year."

"You have so many hot chicks to choose from, man, I'm jealous," Wes said.

"Yeah, but you get Madeline Brescoll. She's smokin'." Even back then I'd heard of Madeline. Everyone in Brockton knew the Brescoll family.

"Speaking of hotties, didn't those cheerleaders want to hang out? Do you have their numbers?" Wes asked Jace.

"That's right." Jace scrolled through his cell phone and pressed 'send'. He got up to walk while he chatted with someone on the other end. I watched him laugh and raise his arm to run a hand through his jet black hair. It was still wet, and it dripped down his muscular back and tan chest. He'd filled out over the past year, and had probably grown half a foot since last summer.

He was usually training for football or meeting up with a girl, and I'd seen a lot less of him than I usually did over the summers. I watched his tight bum as he walked slowly down the edge of the pool. He must do a million squats. Jace turned around when he got to the other side of the pool and ended the call. As he walked towards us, I admired his firm chest, hairless except for a light dusting from his belly button to the edge of his swim trunks. I wanted to trace the V that led invitingly beneath his shorts.

My eyes darted back to my book and I swallowed hard, my mouth suddenly dry. My heart beat rapidly in my chest. I was completely alarmed by the direction of my thoughts. I had never wanted to do anything like that before and I feared that he would somehow know, be able to hear my thoughts or read it on my face. Maybe not seeing him every day like I usually did had changed my perception. Or maybe I'd gotten too much sun. My desire to touch my best friend felt very wrong and I hoped it was temporary.

I continued staring at my book, scanning the pages but not processing anything. I was incredibly thankful I had sunglasses on to help hide my expression. I couldn't look up when Jace settled into the chair next to me.

"They're coming over," he said.

"Sweet. I'll let my mom know." Wes headed inside and I was alone with Jace. For the first time ever, I felt awkward with him.

"I can't believe we're gonna be in different schools this year," he said. "It's gonna suck."

I didn't know if he was talking about me, or Wes, or all three of us. "Yeah. Eighth grade's supposed to be awesome, ruling junior high and all that, but I'm not going to have any friends."

"What do you mean?" I looked at Jace; he was frowning. "What about Tina and Dana? Aren't they in your grade?"

I shrugged. "Yeah, they're okay I guess." I didn't like Tina and Dana. They were obsessed with boys and clothes and gossip, and -- "They're kind of mean," I told Jace.

"They're mean to you?" Jace sat up and clenched his fists. He's always had a quick temper.

"Not to me. They trash-talk everyone else though. It's stupid. They really aren't all that great but everyone thinks they're *so* cool. I don't know why they want to be friends with me. But they always talk to me and invite me to do stuff with them. I bet they think they'll get to know you if they know me." Jace raised his eyebrows. "Because you're sooooo hot," I said sarcastically, mimicking the way other girls sounded when they talked about him. "Or Wes," I quickly added, remembering that I now knew exactly what Tina and Dana had been goin on about. "He's sooooo dreamy."

"Maybe you can make some new friends in your grade this year," Jace offered.

"Yeah, maybe." Jace would have no problem making new friends, and I was terrified he'd forget all about me.

"Are we gonna stay friends?" I asked quietly.

"Hell yes." He sat on the edge of his chair with his hands on his knees and gave me his serious look, which made his green eyes darken. "Pep, you're my best friend. Even more than Wes. You're like family, you know?"

"Yeah. Gran sure thinks of you like a grandson."

"Tell Buns I'm still comin' over all the time for dinner. My dad's cooking is shit and I gotta eat good if I wanna be starting quarterback."

"You think you can? I mean, I know you're really good and you're pretty big for a freshman, but isn't the starter that dude, Reese something? He's a senior now, isn't he?"

"Yeah, he's good. But you'll see. I trained my ass off this summer. Coach is fair. If I'm good enough, I'll get to play."

Wes came back outside, followed by three girls. One of them giggled like an idiot when she saw Jace. I rolled my eyes under my sunglasses. Jace stood up and hugged each girl like he knew them really well. "This is Pepper." Jace gestured to me and I waved from my chair.

"Hi." I noticed Jace didn't introduce the girls and he looked relieved when they told me their names. I wondered if he had them listed on his phone as "the blonde," "big boobs" and "too much make-up." I tucked it away as some good teasing material for later.

"So, how do you guys know each other?" I asked.

"Oh! We've been practicing cheer all week and Jace has been at football so we met at school the other day," the girl named Stacy told me. "I live down the street so when Jace called, we just walked on over!"

I nodded. I was slightly alarmed by the energy bubbling from these girls and I really didn't like the way that Jace was looking at them.

"Did you guys bring your suits? We have hoops for pool basketball," Wes suggested.

The girls eagerly took off their clothes to reveal their bikini-clad bodies. I was wearing a bikini too, but I didn't fill it out like they did. The boys eyed them appreciatively and I felt very small and plain. I wondered if my body would ever fill out. I wondered if Jace would ever look at me like he was looking at those girls.

"Do you wanna play, Pep?" Jace asked, spinning the basketball on the tip of his finger.

"Nah, I want to keep reading. I'm at a really good part," I lied. I had no idea what was happening in the book I was so engrossed in moments ago.

I watched discreetly from the protection of my sunglasses as the boys played basketball against the girls. They touched each other frequently and unnecessarily. My chest felt tight and my entire body was tense. The physical reaction startled me and it took a few minutes before I realized it was a manifestation of my feelings. I was angry. And jealous. These girls didn't know Jace, yet he was letting them touch him.

When Jace took one of the girls to the pool shed I felt like crying. Wrapping a towel around myself, I walked inside the house while Wes continued flirting with the other two girls in the pool. Without my own cell phone, I had to ask Mrs. Jamison if I could use their landline to call Gran. Jace would be annoyed when I left without telling him, but I didn't care.

I waited outside for Gran. When she saw me, she didn't ask any questions -- she could see that I was upset. After dinner, she made my favorite dessert – banana bread pudding - and we watched Titanic for the hundredth time. And when Jace called after dinner asking for me, she didn't need to say anything. She knew.

"She's not feeling good," Gran said gruffly on the phone.

Jace said something on the other end and Gran replied, "It's woman stuff, Jace."

I figured that would shut him up, but apparently not. Jace must've kept asking, because Gran said, "She's fine. Cramps."

I couldn't help but smile. Anyone else might be embarrassed by her but I love her like crazy.

"Mmmhmm," she responded, and mmmhmmmed a few more times. "Okay, young man, we'll see ya for dinner then. Don't cause too much trouble on your first day, ya hear?" She laughed at something he said before hanging up.

"Jace's gonna keep comin' for dinner after his practices like usual." Gran sat next to me on the couch and patted my knee. "It ain't all gonna change, baby girl."

But it already had.

★ ★ ★

After Jace leaves, I push play on my iPod and lie down on my bed. I let my body melt into my comforter and close my eyes.

I can't deny my body's response to Jace. He's hot as all hell. And we like each other. As friends. So what's the problem, right? Why not try being more than friends? Or at least friends with benefits, as so many like to term their non-relationships?

The problem is that Jace thinks of me like his little sister. Last year I was coming out of the girl's locker room after track practice and I stopped at the water fountain. Jace was in the locker room talking to his best guy friend, Remy Laroche. They play baseball in the spring. I'd heard that guys didn't give me much attention because Jace warned them away. I wanted to believe he did this because he wanted me for himself, but, based on the way he acted around me, I feared it was something else. Turns out I was right. Worse than being friend-zoned... I was *like family.*

Yup, that's what he said. Remy asked Jace why he didn't like other guys showing an interest in me, and if he wasn't going to let other guys hook up with me, why didn't he get with me himself?

I was clutching the water fountain, but I wasn't drinking. I stayed leaning forward though, letting the stream of water brush my lips. Then I heard Jace's voice.

"Man, that's not gonna happen. Pepper's my family. She's like my sister."

His *sister.*

Okay, so he could have just been *saying* that, right? Maybe he didn't really mean it. Doubtful.

There's no question Jace *really* likes girls. I'm a girl, and we've been alone in his room, or mine, tons of times and he's never made a pass. So, the only other explanation is that he doesn't want me because I'm just not hot enough.

Look, I know I'm no Madeline Brescoll, but I'm not ugly. My boobs are fairly unimpressive but I've got great legs. Despite Jace's efforts, some guys *have* shown an interest in me. Given Jace's reputation with the ladies, it seems like he would have made a move... if he didn't think of me like his sister, that is. So there you have it.

Sure, I think of Jace like family in some ways too. We love each other unconditionally. We've got each other's backs. He's got his own crowd at school, and I've got mine. But we know we'll hang out together on our own time. I don't have any siblings, but maybe that's what it's like.

Unfortunately, my stupid libido doesn't get that she's not supposed to want Jace.

Chapter 3

The next morning I hop in to the passenger side of Jace's black Jeep for the first day of school. The sound of Green Day is pulsing through the car.

I hand Jace the cinnamon raisin bagel with cream cheese that Gran made for him. "What's up?" I ask before taking a bite of my own bagel.

"You and your short-ass shorts." Jace shakes his head in disapproval.

Ignoring him, I roll down the window. Why should I hide my legs, my best feature? With my arm out the window, my hand slices through the warm breeze.

When I feel Jace staring at me at a stoplight, I ask, "What?"

He reaches out and swipes cream cheese from the corner of my mouth with his index finger before putting it in his own mouth to lick it.

My mouth goes dry. Ugh. Does he have any idea what he does to me with a simple gesture like that? I sigh and look back out the window, trying to take my mind off his green eyes that scream sex and mischief.

As we pull into the senior parking lot at Brockton Public, the groups mingling around outside turn their heads. Everyone recognizes Jace's car.

Kayla Chambers, Andrea Hill, and Lisa Delany greet Jace on the sidewalk. They're all seniors this year and, as usual, look gorgeous wearing summer dresses that show off tan arms, legs, and cleavage. I finger my own long brown hair that hangs well past my shoulders. They smile indulgently at me. Not as fake as Madeline, but it's no secret they'd ignore me completely if I didn't know Jace.

I walk towards the school and feel a familiar arm settle around my shoulder. "Morning, Pepper."

"Hey, Charlie." He opens the door and gestures for me to go inside before him. Charlie Owens is the captain of the boys' cross team and is one of my closest friends.

"So, did you get to meet your hero yesterday?" I ask him.

Charlie laughs. "Yeah, yeah."

Zoe pops up next to us. "You mean his man-crush? It's totally justified, Charles. Ryan Harding is, like, really hot. And he's actually super cool. For a cross country runner, that is. I bet you he gets scooped up by the Barbies though."

"The Barbies?" I ask. I stop at my locker and start turning the combination.

"Oh, don't pretend you don't know what I mean. The hot popular girls. You know." Zoe nods her head enthusiastically. "I mean, you could be one too if you wanted, Pepper."

"A Barbie? Is that supposed to be an insult or a compliment? I'm not even blonde." I pull a couple of books from my backpack to store in my locker.

"Whatever, I was just calling them Barbies anyway. That's not like, what everyone else calls them, you know. I made it up. You like?" Without pausing for a breath, Zoe turns her attention to Charlie. "So Charlie, I didn't get to talk to you after the cookout. What did you think? Ryan's cool, right?" I don't know how the girl has so much energy this early in the morning, but she is always buzzing. It's contagious. I suppose that's why I like her so much.

Charlie scratches his head, and a lock of curly blonde hair falls over his forehead. "Sure, yeah, he's a nice guy. He won't have anyone to train with, though. I feel kind of bad. Even his easy pace on the team run yesterday was quick, and I'm pretty sure he was making an effort to go slow."

Zoe tugs on one of her pigtail braids. She has the most beautiful strawberry blonde hair, but she rarely wears it down. "Yeah, well, that's what Pepper has to do when she runs with the team."

Zoe Burton is the reason I started running freshman year. We sat next to each other in freshman English on the first day of school and she talked me into showing up at the first cross practice.

"Yeah, but she can at least do speed workouts with the guys' team. Ryan's going to be doing all the workouts by himself," Charlie points out.

"He's probably used to it," I tell them.

"Workouts" for runners doesn't mean exactly what most people think. A "run" is just that – a regular old run. We run every day, but we have "workouts" about twice a week. Workouts require faster running, intervals, hills, or something more specific that is harder than a regular run. We also do a long run or a race once a week.

Zoe twirls her braided pigtail around her finger and changes the subject. "I'm sorry you had to miss the cookout at Coach's yesterday. How was Bunny's birthday party?"

"Well, we had like twenty people over to her friend Lulu's house. I think Gran's got half of them convinced they need a medical marijuana prescription and the other half already have one. The women got Gran a bong for her birthday. And then they christened it." I glance up at Zoe and Charlie.

Zoe's mouth is slightly ajar and Charlie is slowly shaking his head back and forth. They've met Gran before, so this can't be a huge shock, but still. "So yeah, I'm pretty sure I was high from secondhand smoke by the time I had to drive Gran home after the party."

Zoe's eyes widen as she zeroes in on someone behind me. "Oh, hi Jace," she squeaks.

"Hi, Zoe." Jace leans against the locker next to mine and nods at Charlie. "Charlie." Charlie raises his hand in a half wave. The Barbies linger behind Jace.

"So you got high yesterday, huh?" he asks me.

"Shut up." I punch his arm. Hard as a rock.

The bell rings for first period. I shut my locker. "Anyone got Ramirez for History?"

Zoe raises her hand and we head down the hallway.

"Drive you home after practice, Pepper," Jace calls out.

I raise my hand in a wave.

"How do you sit in the car with him every day without jumping him? I mean, I get turned on just looking at the guy," Zoe whispers loudly.

"It's not easy, Zoe. It's not easy."

When I walk into the cafeteria, I recognize Ryan Harding immediately. He's sitting on a windowsill by the popular table, with Lisa and her long blonde hair leaning up very close to him, batting her big blue eyes. She really does look like a Barbie.

I know what Ryan Harding looks like because he was featured in *Running Fast Magazine* last month. He won high school Nationals as a junior, and is shooting for a second win this year. The article focused on his decision to move to Brockton for his senior year, instead of staying in California. His dad, Mark Harding, was the new head coach at the University of Colorado last year. Ryan was planning to stay with his uncle and finish up high school in California, even though his parents and little brother moved here. I read the whole article, because I was curious about the guy. Plus, I want to go to UC, so Mark might be my coach someday.

I realize that I'm staring, and Ryan has caught me. The corners of his mouth lift and he pushes off the windowsill. Lisa stumbles backward, and I can't stop my smile. She really irritates me.

When Ryan walks my way, I look behind me to see if there's someone else he's approaching. But when I turn back around, Ryan is standing right in front of me. "Hi, Pepper," he says warmly. "I'm Ryan."

"I know. I mean, you were on a magazine cover so I know what you look like. But, um, we've never met. I would remember." I shake my head, and can't help but chuckle at how dumb I sound. Starstruck. I'm as bad as Charlie. "Um. Yeah. So, anyway, how do you know who I am? I'm not on any magazine covers, as far as I know."

Ryan laughs and shrugs. "Someone pointed you out earlier today. Sorry, I don't mean to be creepy. I thought I'd meet you yesterday. At the cookout thing."

"Oh yeah, I was bummed to miss it. It was my Grandma's birthday party. But I'll be at practice today." I become aware that we are standing in the middle of the cafeteria, and that Lisa is shooting daggers in my direction. I feel others' eyes on me as I start walking towards Charlie's table.

He's sitting with Claire Padilla, my co-captain, and the rest of our crew. "You've met Charlie, right?" I nod towards Charlie, who waves tentatively. "He was the guys' number one runner last year. He's a senior with you."

"Oh yeah, we met yesterday. Hey, Charlie." He puts up his fist and the two do the pound thing.

I plop down next to Charlie and notice Ryan watching me uncertainly. "Wanna join us?" I ask.

"Oh, my lunch is back there." He points behind him with his thumb. "Let me just go grab it." He hurries over to the popular table and I catch Jace staring in my direction, along with everyone else at his table.

"Wow, he came right up to you. I guess he knew who you were," Charlie says excitedly.

"I guess. He said someone pointed me out to him, whatever that means."

"Probably did his research on Coach Tom and the team before deciding whether to train with us. You know, as the reigning state champ, you're kind of famous, too." He bites into his sandwich.

I shrug and turn to my other side. "Hey Claire, what's up? We didn't see you much this summer." She and Zoe are the number two and three runners on the team, depending on the day.

"I was studying for the SAT," she explains. Claire's a senior, and has been obsessed with college admissions since I met her my freshman year.

"All summer, every day?"

"Well, when I wasn't studying, I was running or working at the pool."

Ryan sits down between Claire and me. "Are you a lifeguard?" he asks.

Claire blushes and swallows. "Yes," she whispers.

"What about you, Pepper? What did you do this summer?" Ryan turns his attention to me.

"Oh, I bus tables at Old House Tavern."

I feel a hand squeeze my shoulder and I know immediately who it is. "Hi, Jace."

He pulls over an empty chair and manages to squeeze it between Ryan and me. "Pepper," he says in greeting.

I have no idea what he's doing here. He never sits with me at lunch.

"Um, have you met Ryan? He's a senior on the cross team."

Jace laughs darkly. "Yeah, Pepper. We met."

"You did? When?"

Ryan answers, "At a party last night. Lisa Delany lives on my street, saw me moving in, and introduced me to a bunch of people."

"Oh." I don't go to parties. It must have been after the cookout.

"What'd Bunny pack you for lunch?" Jace asks while poking through my red polka-dotted lunch box. I really like polka dots.

"Why? Are you going to steal it?"

"Depends what it is. Hmmm. . . banana. Nope. Sandwich. Looks like. . . peanut butter and jelly? String cheese. Wait." He pauses dramatically. "No way." He pulls out a Tupperware container. "Are these ants on a log?"

"Maybe," I tell him sheepishly.

"What are ants on a log?" Ryan asks over Jace's shoulder.

I open the Tupperware and hold one up. "See? Celery, peanut butter, and raisins on top. My Gran's been making these for me since I was five."

Jace pats my cheek. "I won't steal them. Don't worry. You need to fuel up. You've gotta get strong to kick some ass again this year." He wraps his big hand around my puny arm. "Hmmm. . .. kinda scrawny, Pep, maybe you should incorporate push-ups into your routine."

I pull away from him, embarrassed. Not because my biceps are small, but because his touch on my bare arm feels really nice. And people are watching. "I do push-ups, Jace. And I'll ask Gran to make you some ants on a log for lunch tomorrow if you want."

He smiles at me. "Thanks." He pushes away from the chair and stands up. Then he leans down and kisses me on the top of the head before walking back to the popular table. I roll my eyes and bite into my peanut butter and jelly sandwich.

Ryan, Charlie, Claire, and the three other runners at the table are all staring at me. "What?"

Claire whispers. "Uh, Jace Wilder just kissed you."

Rollie, who is sitting across from me, says, "Yeah, and in front of everyone. Like, *everyone* was watching. He *never* comes over here." Rollie's real name is Roland Fowler. His nickname has nothing to do with his body type because he's incredibly lanky.

"It's nothing, guys. He's just comfortable with me because we've known each other forever. My Gran used to babysit him and he lives down the street." They all know this already, except for Ryan, so I don't quite understand their reactions.

They are still staring at me when I poke my straw into my chocolate milk. "It was on the top of my head, you guys, jeez!"

I'm thankful when Charlie changes the subject. "So, wouldn't it be badass if both the guys' and girls' teams made state this year?"

"You have to get first or second as a team at Districts, right?" Ryan asks.

"Yup," Rollie answers. "Both guys and girls got third at Districts the past two years."

"And Claire and Charlie just barely missed qualifying individually last year," I add.

Only ten teams in Colorado qualify for State as a team; everyone else has to qualify individually.

"We don't want poor Pepper to have to go to State all alone again this year," Charlie teases. "Although I'm sure Ryan will be going."

There's not much of a question that I'll make it to the State meet. I made it the past two years, and won last year. The real question is whether I will qualify for Regionals at State, and then if I'll go on to Nationals.

"We're all going to State, both teams," I say with confidence. "I just know this is going to be an epic season."

Chapter 4

Fifteen minutes into our warm-up jog, and it's only me, Claire Zoe, and a freshman girl I just met named Jenny Mendoza. Another group of girls jogs behind us and then it thins out. This is what usually happens at the first official practice of the season, since most people don't run much over the summer and struggle through the warm-up run. We're not going very fast. I tried to keep it at an easy conversational pace, but it looks like we'll really only have one more top scorer on varsity this year. Claire and Zoe are fast, and Jenny could be fast. She looks comfortable jogging with us.

"Holy hell," Zoe exclaims. "Check out the football field. Jace is taking his shirt off. And his butt looks so freaking good in those tight little whatever pants-shorts things they wear. Oh wow. Six pack. Wow. Just wow. I would pay to touch him. I would. I swear."

Claire has gone scarlet, as usual when Zoe starts gushing. I glance at Jenny. She's grinning.

"Yeah. I think I'm going to like high school. Can we make a point of running by the football field during every practice?"

I laugh. "Sure, Jenny."

"Jace kissed Pepper in the cafeteria today," Claire blurts out.

"What?!" Zoe screeches. A couple of guys on the football field look our way.

"Zoe, chill. It was a peck on my head after I told him I'd ask Gran to make him ants on a log for lunch. You know how it is with him."

"Whatever. I'm jealous. He's totally got a soft spot for you and everyone knows it." Zoe is so dramatic.

I ignore her. We reconvene by the baseball field after the warm-up. It's hot out, and the boys have taken off their shirts. I can't help but check out Ryan, whose sandy brown hair ruffles in the breeze.

He's lean and muscular, and far from scrawny like some of the cross guys are. Zoe and Claire strip off their tee shirts, and I follow suit. Jenny watches us.

"Hmmm. . . I'll have to remember not to wear a white sports bra next time it's a hot day out," she observes. Yes. Hot days and the shirts go flying --along with the teenage hormones.

Coach Tom is wearing his favorite Rockies baseball hat as he gives the same welcoming speech I've heard for the past two years. "All right, guys!" he calls to get our attention. "Yesterday was the social welcoming, and today is the training welcome. Some of you are brand new to cross country. Here's what you need to know. We don't cut anyone. If you make it to the practices you can race in the meets. However, only seven girls and seven boys are on varsity." He holds up seven fingers to emphasize the point. "Varsity-only races are marked with a star on the team calendar. Only varsity goes to Districts and State, and that's if they qualify. Looks like we have about thirty girls here today, and forty boys. Everyone who was on varsity last year, or who wants to try for it this year, will come with me. Everyone else will go with our assistant coach, Janet. We'll start dividing you up into groups based on your pace, but for today you'll have to make your own decision about where you think you'll fit in."

When I look around, I see a lot of panicked expressions. It's like this every year, too. I'd shown up to my first practice freshman year wearing high top Converse sneakers and jean shorts, and got more than a few funny looks. It didn't seem like a hard decision which group to run with the first day -- I'd either keep up or I wouldn't. It's not like anyone would be tackling me. There was no doubt in my mind that first day that I belonged in Janet's group, but after rocking the hill sprints in my high tops, I'd been moved to Coach Tom's group. I've been working out with him ever since.

Coach explains that our group is doing mile repeats, which he has measured off with orange cones around the baseball field and up a hill towards the parking lot. "It's a hilly mile loop. Zoe and Claire will lead the girls' group. Three by one mile repeats with three minutes rest in between each mile. Try for about a 6:15 pace. I don't expect everyone to keep up. Just do your best. Charlie and Pepper, I'd like you to lead the guys out at 5:45 pace. You'll be doing four miles total. Ryan, you're starting thirty seconds behind the guys' group, and you'll try to catch them by the end of the mile, so about a 5:15 pace."

I tighten my ponytail and head over to the first cone with Charlie. "Ready, guys?" he calls to the fifteen guys behind us. We start our watches and set off.

The rest of the guys settle in behind us. They know not to question our pace. The last interval will be fair game, but Coach instructed me and Charlie to set the pace, and that means everyone has to stay behind us for the first three miles. I'm usually in the lead at races, so Coach knows it's important for me to get familiar with pacing, even if it does piss off some of the guys who don't like following a girl.

Ryan runs past us at the end of each mile, before we take the three-minute break between each one. He looks so strong and relaxed running a five-minute pace, it's hard not to admire him. Charlie and Rollie outkick me on the last one, but I'm not far behind. My legs are tired, my chest burns a little, and I love it.

After showering in the locker room and changing back into my school clothes, I wait on the hood of Jace's Jeep. I pull out *The Catcher in the Rye* from my backpack, the book assigned for English, and start reading the first chapter.

"Hey Pepper, good workout today." I look up to find Ryan standing in front of me, his hair still damp from a shower.

"Thanks," I say, putting a finger in the book to mark my place. "What do you think? Training with a new team, I mean."

"Oh, it seems cool. I didn't really have any guys to do workouts with last year anyway, so I like the way Coach Tom did it today. Plus you guys have a ton of people on the team." He smiles at that. "Seems like people are really into cross around here."

"Yeah, it's pretty popular. I mean, UC's here, and they've got one of the best teams in the NCAA, so people are into the running scene. But it's not exactly the cool team to be on. I'm sure that's not news to you."

Ryan laughs. "Yeah, it's only cool if it involves tackling each other, right?"

"Something like that," I say, nodding toward the football team.

"When I talked to Coach on the phone before moving out here, he told me that you would be shooting for Nationals too. That's awesome. How come you didn't go last year?"

I shrug. "The State meet was my goal last year. I hadn't really thought beyond that."

"I'm excited someone on my team has the same goals as me," Ryan says, as though it's a forgone conclusion that I'll qualify for Nationals.

I raise an eyebrow at him. "I'm thinking your goal is to win again. And mine is just to qualify."

"Oh, you'll make it." I wish I were as sure of that as he seems to be. "Anyway, is this your Jeep?"

"It's Jace's. I'm waiting for him to give me a ride home."

"I can give you a ride; where do you live?"

"Near campus. But really, he's on my street, so it's easy."

"I live near campus, too. I can give you rides home after practice whenever you want."

That would be convenient. We end practice at the same time, and football usually goes longer. But for some reason, I don't want to sacrifice that time with Jace. It's *our* time. Without the Barbies or his friends hanging around.

I give Ryan an evasive answer, "Yeah, maybe, but Jace usually eats dinner at my house anyway, so I'd have to wait on him here or there before eating either way. I'll let you know, though."

"Looks like football's out." He nods towards the other end of the parking lot, where a group of muddy shirtless guys are walking our way. "See you tomorrow, Pepper."

"See you." I smile at him and hop down from the hood.

I can't help but stare at Jace while he walks toward me with his teammates. He's changed into shorts that hang low on his hips, and his tan chest is glistening with sweat. He didn't take the time to shower, and Gran's going to give him a hard time if he sits down at the dinner table like that.

My eyes make their way to his face and he breaks into a grin when our eyes lock. I look down and busy myself putting my book back in my backpack. It's not like the boy doesn't know he's hot. And I am female. But still. It's not like that between us. And I'm ashamed he caught me checking him out. What is with me today and checking out boys?

I hear the Jeep beep unlocked and I open the passenger side door and jump in. When we pull up outside my apartment building ten minutes later, Jace leaves the car running.

"You're not coming in for dinner?" I try to keep the disappointment out of my voice.

"Can't. I have an errand to run," he says.

I open the door and wait for further explanation. I want to ask him what the errand is, but I know that if he wanted me to know, he would have told me.

"So, no Hendrix puzzle later?"

"Sorry, Pep. I got this thing I can't get out of," Jace tells me, being vague as usual. He's keeping me out of his social life. It's nothing new. I only know a little about it from the school gossip.

"Yeah, okay," I say, resigned. My guess is he's going to hook up with a girl. I know he does this with lots of girls, but it still makes me queasy. And I know why they call it heartbreak. It's weird; my heart does actually hurt a little every time I think of him with another girl.

"I can get a ride home with someone on the team now, who lives near us. So, you don't have to give me a ride home anymore," I tell him as I get out of the Jeep.

It's petty, I know. But I don't want him to think I'm some obligation. And I want to know if he actually likes coming over for dinner and sitting in the car with me. Maybe it's just a habit for him, and it's easier to stick with than quit. After all, it's his senior year. He might have better things to do.

"Who?" Jace turns the full force of his green eyes on me, narrowing them slightly.

"The new kid. Ryan," I tell him.

Jace looks ahead out the windshield and clenches his jaw. I don't think he likes Ryan and I'm not sure why. It feels like five minutes pass before Jace turns back to me. "Do you want to ride with him?"

I shrug. "It just seems easier, you know, since our practices end at the same time. And then if you have stuff to do after practice, you don't have to worry about it."

"Whatever. If that's what you wanna do." He turns up the radio, indicating that the conversation is over.

I take the not-so-subtle hint and head inside.

Gran's made coconut cream pie for dessert and it's Jace's favorite. "I'll wrap up a piece for you to bring him tomorrow," she says.

My mood lifts when I flip through my running journal after dinner. I've been writing down my workouts for over a year now. I know that we did the exact same workout from today at some point last season. And it was the same mile loop on the baseball field, too.

I find the page from last September with my mile splits and I compare them to my splits from this year. I'm already a little faster, and it's only August. Coach mostly just had me doing easy base mileage all summer. Today was my first real speed workout of the season and I'm in great shape.

I pull out my calendar and count thirty-six days until my first meet. I'm skipping all of the September races and my first race is the Aspen Leaf Invitational in October. After that is Districts, the first weekend in November. State is the weekend before Thanksgiving, and I need to place in the top seven to qualify for Regionals. While I don't think I should have much trouble placing in the top seven at State, I want to win it a second year in a row.

The last Saturday in November is Regionals, and that's when I really have to throw down the hammer. If all goes well, I'll be racing at Nationals in December. Until then, I need to focus on staying healthy, not getting injured, and sticking to the training plan. And the plan does not include Jace Wilder.

Chapter 5

Ryan Harding is waiting by my locker the next morning. "Hey Ryan, what's up?" I greet him, wondering what he's doing here.

"Not much. I was hoping to catch you." He leans on the locker next to mine as I play with my combination.

"How'd you know this was my locker?"

"Oh, I was talking to Charlie this morning, and I asked him."

I take a peek at him. His hands are shoved into his shorts pockets, a pair of worn dark khakis that are slightly frayed at the bottoms. With a light blue tee shirt that accentuates his tan, he looks good. I notice girls checking him out as they walk by.

He clears his throat. "So, are you going to the party tomorrow night?"

School started on a Thursday this year, so the weekend has already arrived. "No, I don't really party." He must not have gotten the memo about me.

"Really?" He looks genuinely surprised. "Oh." He pauses for a beat while I close up my locker. "Do you not like them? I was kind of hoping you'd go with me."

I smile at him. "I don't know if I like them. I've never been."

He follows along while I walk to my first class. "You should at least go to one. See what it's all about. You know, part of the high school experience."

I chuckle. "I'm surprised that the cross country national champ is peer-pressuring me like this. How can you stay focused if you party?" I shake my head at him. "I don't go to the parties myself, but I hear enough about them to know that they're not exactly in line with my training plan."

"Yeah, I'm sure they aren't too different from San Diego parties. But don't you need to have a little fun in high school? I'd go crazy if all I did was think about running."

"I've heard the speech about balance before, but I see what you're saying. I do have fun." An idea occurs to me. "Why don't you hang out with some of us this weekend? I usually spend time with people on the cross team that you've already met."

We're standing at the door to my Spanish classroom. I glance at him, curious if he'll find an excuse to bail. After all, my group of friends doesn't even register on the popularity totem pole, and he is already being scoped out by Lisa, who's at the top of the high school food chain.

"That would be great." Ryan smiles and his blue eyes crinkle. Boy, he is really cute.

I'm momentarily distracted when I feel my stomach flutter. I blink quickly and look away to avoid his gaze, then rush to fill the silence. "Anyway, I wanted to take you up on that offer for a ride after practice."

"That's great!" He seems genuinely enthusiastic about it, and opens his mouth to say something else, but the bell rings for first period and he changes tack. "See you at lunch? Which period do you have lunch today?"

"Uh, B I think?"

"Oh, I'm A. . . .. so I guess practice then. See you later!" We wave at each other as I head into my classroom.

I find myself thinking about Ryan throughout the day. I'm excited to see him at practice. We have a five-mile recovery run from yesterday's workout and I'm disappointed that the boys and girls run in separate groups on our easy days. I keep sneaking peeks at Ryan while we stretch out after the run. His shirt is off, and I can see his abs contracting as he does sit-ups and push-ups. I'm having trouble concentrating on my own exercises.

"He's really hot, huh?" Dorothy Sandoval asks. She's doing lunges next to me, and her eyes are on Ryan.

"Yeah," I say evasively, forcing myself to look away from him. I'm wary around Dorothy. She's the only other senior aside from Claire on varsity this year, but she doesn't hang out with our group. Dorothy is friends with a group that Zoe refers to as the "wannabes." These girls go to all the parties, and do whatever it is they think they're supposed to do to be cool, but they're still a step below the most popular group of seniors in the social hierarchy.

Dorothy's never been rude to me, but her agenda is fairly transparent and not something I want to be a part of. Her attitude wouldn't bother me if it didn't impact the cross team. She's got a lot of talent, but is really inconsistent in her workouts and at races. I think her main goal with running is to keep her body looking good. She doesn't seem to care if her social agenda with boyfriends and parties interferes with her running performance.

"I hear he's been hanging out with Jace's crowd. I hung out with him at Lisa Delany's party last weekend. I think he was happy that someone on the cross team was there. I bet we'll be really good friends." Dorothy doesn't take her eyes off of him as she chats. I can see the predatory look in her eyes as she imagines her plan unfolding. Ryan could be her "in" to the Barbie group.

"Mmmhmm," is all I say in response.

I finish my last set of strength exercises and move towards Zoe and Claire to avoid any further conversation with Dorothy.

"What's the plan for this weekend?" I ask them.

"It's Friday. I thought we'd go to the first football game of the year," Zoe replies.

"And we have our long run tomorrow. Do you guys want to meet at my house to do yoga after?" Claire offers.

As we make plans, the guys join in our conversation. "Are you running with us tomorrow, Pepper?" Charlie asks.

"No, Coach wants me doing long runs with the girls for now." I like running with the girls' group, but it requires me to back off from the faster pace my legs always seem to want to go. Which I guess is the point. For now, at least.

"You guys want to come over to my place on Saturday night?" Rollie asks. The Fowlers have a huge house and Rollie is an only child. It's the best place for us to hang out at.

We make arrangements to carpool to the football game later tonight, and plan to meet at Rollie's house late afternoon tomorrow, after we've done our long run and yoga at Claire's place.

"Do we have to meet so freakin' early?" Dorothy complains.

"Nine isn't that early," Zoe says. "And we're meeting two minutes from your house. I think you can handle it."

"Look, it's the first football game of the season, and the party afterward is going to be raging. You guys might be going to bed at a reasonable hour but I don't plan to. Why can't we just go a little later?" she whines.

"Dorothy, it's supposed to be a high of ninety-five tomorrow. Do you really want to run for an hour and a half when it gets that hot out?" I ask her.

"Besides," Jenny pipes up, "all the big meets are in the morning, so we should at least do some of our runs early to get used to it."

I smile at her. Good point.

"Fine." Dorothy crosses her arms moodily. She loses the scowl quickly when she sees Ryan approach. He was talking to Coach during the weekend planning conversation.

"You shower here, right, Pepper? Do you want to meet by my car after?" Ryan asks.

I can feel Dorothy's eyes on me.

"I usually only shower here because I'm waiting on Jace. We can leave now if you'd rather do that."

"As long as you don't mind a stinky car ride with me," he counters.

"It's your car. And we'll stink together so it's cool. Your windows roll down, right?" I tease.

Ryan has almost the exact same Jeep as Jace, except it's green instead of black, and it's an automatic instead of a standard.

"A bunch of us are going to the game tonight if you want to come," I tell him.

"Oh yeah? I already told a couple guys I'd meet them for pizza beforehand, but maybe I'll see you there."

"Let me guess. You're meeting at Lou's?"

"That's the place. Why? Is it good?"

"Yup. Best pizza in town. I like the deep dish crust but they've got thin crust too if that's your style." Just the thought of it makes me hungry. "Who are you meeting?"

"You know Remy Laroche and Ben Hughes?"

"Yeah, of course. I mean, we're not friends. But I know who they are." They're the captains of the boys' soccer team and two of the most popular guys in school, along with Jace and Connor, who captain the football team.

"Are you going to the party with them afterward?" I'm curious. We have a long run in the morning, and the boys are meeting even earlier than we are. How does he juggle it?

"Nah. One party a weekend is enough for me." He grins in my direction. "I'll check out the one happening on Saturday night. Sunday's my sleep-in day anyway."

"We're getting together at Rollie's place tomorrow. It'll just be a few of us. He's got a pool and a ping-pong table. You should come."

Now that I know Jace's group is recruiting him, I seriously doubt he'll hang out with us. But it can't hurt to ask.

"That'd be cool. Here, put my number in your phone and give me a call when you're ready to go over tomorrow. I can pick you up."

After I put his number in my phone he asks me who's going to be at Rollie's.

"Most of the guys' team, probably. Chris, Matt and Charlie, who are seniors with you. And then Rollie, obviously, and Omar, who are both juniors with me."

"Oh yeah, I met Omar at that party at Lisa's house the other night. Cool guy. He plays baseball with Remy and Jace in the spring, right?"

"Yup, that's him." Omar Hernandez is the only one in our group who doesn't do track in the spring. It's kind of fun having one of our own to root for at baseball games but I think we embarrass him a bit with our enthusiastic cheering. Dorothy was actually wrong about being the only one on the cross team at Lisa's party. Omar's got a whole other group of friends he hangs out with sometimes who are much cooler than us, and he's not a jerk about it like she is.

"What about the girls?"

"Just me, Claire, and Zoe. The other girls who train with us are cool but we don't really hang out with them too much outside practice."

"What about Dorothy?" he asks.

"Dorothy?" I can't hide my surprise. I totally thought she was exaggerating when she said they'd be good friends.

"Yeah, sorry if she's your friend, but she's, uh, a bit much," Ryan says sheepishly.

I laugh. "No worries. I'm not really friends with her so you don't have to feel bad. I'm sure she'll be at that party you were going to go to."

Ryan scratches the back of his head. "Sorry. It's just, she kind of made a pass at me the other night at Lisa's party. I don't think she's gotten the hint that I'm not interested like that. It's sort of awkward."

I can't help laughing again. I can definitely picture Dorothy throwing herself at him. "Lucky you. I don't think she's going to give up easily."

Ryan is easy to talk to and the drive home flies by. There's no doubt Dorothy will have competition from other girls seeking his attention. Maybe even me.

Chapter 6

Ryan fits in great with my group of friends, but he also manages somehow to establish himself as one of the most popular guys in school. We had a ton of fun hanging out on Saturday night, and he's quickly become a good friend.

The following Saturday is the first cross meet of the year, and I'm not racing. Ryan isn't either, which makes it a little easier, but it still feels strange. I show up at the meet to warm up with the team, just like I would for any race, but I don't have a number pinned to my jersey, and I don't toe the starting line with everyone else.

Ryan and I jog next to the course together after the race starts.

"Did your coach back in California take you out of the early season meets like this?" I ask.

"Yeah, after my freshman year. As soon as I had an extended championship season."

The race today isn't an important one, but I can still sense the familiar nervous energy buzzing through the runners and the cheering crowds. "I feel better knowing you're following the same training plan, but it still seems weird to me," I confess.

"I know. I love racing. But you really can't expect your body to hold up through Nationals if you start racing now. You don't want to make it all the way to Nationals, and then find your legs totally trashed because you took out the beginning of the season too hard." He slaps his hands lightly onto his quads. "I did that sophomore year."

"I thought you said your coach started taking you out of early season races that year," I ask, confused.

"He did. But I didn't trust it, so I did extra runs and hard workouts without telling him. I just barely made it to Nationals, and then I got third to last place. I also gave myself stress fractures and had to sit out the track season."

I make a face. Stress fractures suck. "And then the next year you came back and won Nationals. You learned your lesson, I take it?"

"Yeah, that's probably why it's a lot easier for me to sit out this time around." He shrugs. "I've done it, and it worked."

If I'm honest with myself, I might have a little crush on Ryan. I hope I do. He'd be the perfect guy for me to get past Jace. Ryan's adorable, and sweet, and he's been giving me great advice about training and racing. It seems like he could be interested in me in a more-than-friends way, but Dorothy keeps saying that Lisa Delany is gunning for him, and I can't compete with that.

"Do you have any plans for tonight?" he asks. We stop to stretch out near the finish line, where we can cheer for our teammates when they pass in a few minutes.

"No plans. I'll probably just watch a movie or something. You?"

"Remy's having a party. You should come. I can pick you up."

"Are the parties any fun? All I hear about are the hook-ups, the drugs, the drinking... I don't really do any of that stuff. And I doubt I'll know very many people."

"You'll know more than I will. And you don't *have* to do any of that. If you don't have fun, we can leave and watch a movie instead," he suggests.

"Ryan, are you asking me, like, on a date?" He smiles slightly and looks down. "I'm serious. I'm asking because I don't know how these things work. I've never been on a date before. Except to prom with Charlie last year. And that was more as friends." Charlie kissed me that night. It was my first kiss, hardly more than a peck on the lips, and it had been nice. But I didn't really want anything else, and I don't think Charlie wanted our friendship to change either. So that was the extent of my dating experience.

"Do you want it to be a date? It can be, if you want. Or we can just go, you know, as friends, teammates, whatever."

"We'll just leave it at that for now. Ambiguous. But yes. I'll go with you." He grins at me, relief evident on his face. "But I should warn you. You'll have to meet my Gran when you pick me up."

★ ★ ★

Gran insists that Ryan come over for dinner before taking me to the party. When I hear the doorbell ringing I scurry to open it before she can get there.

"Hey, Ryan." Dave wiggles by me and sniffs around Ryan, sizing him up. "Are you okay with dogs?" I ask, reaching down to ease Dave back.

"Yeah." He laughs. "We have a bulldog."

"That's good. The guy sniffing your butt here is Dave. He likes to think he protects me and Gran from intruders but he's harmless."

I notice a bouquet of flowers in Ryan's hand. He follows my eyeline and says, "Oh, I brought these for you and your Gran. You know, for making dinner. My mom made brownies for me to bring, but my little brother ate half of them, so. . ."

I laugh and smell the flowers as he hands them to me. "Thanks, I'll grab a vase."

Gran pokes her head into the entryway holding a spatula in her hand. She's wearing the polka-dot apron I got her for her birthday and one of her matching sweatsuits – orange, this time. Her puppy-dog slippers squeak when she walks towards us.

"Hi there, Ryan! Oh, you brought flowers. I knew I was going to like you. I made lasagna. Do you like lasagna? You aren't a vegetarian, are you? A lot of vegetarians these days. I don't understand it myself. We're carnivores. Why fight nature?"

"No, Mrs. Jones, I'm not a vegetarian," Ryan says, and I can tell he's holding back laughter.

"Mrs. Jones? No one calls me that, dear. It's just Bunny. That's been my name as long as I can recall and that's what you'll call me. Now come on in. Have a seat."

I pull out the chair that Jace usually sits in and gesture for him to get comfy.

"You guys have some great names in your family," Ryan says as he sits down. "Pepper, what's the story behind your name?"

I sit down across from him. "Unfortunately, the only explanation is that my parents were crazy."

"It's true!" Gran calls from the kitchen.

"Yeah, Gran and I have no idea why they picked such a weird name. But it's mine. And they chose it. So I like it." I shrug and take a sip of lemonade. "Is lemonade okay? Do you want milk or soda or some water?" Jace always drinks milk. I don't know what other boys drink.

Gran brings the lasagna into the room and places it in the center of the table. "Now, Ryan dear, I can't give you anything to drink because you're driving, but my baby girl here needs to have a glass of wine."

"Gran!" I exclaim. "I don't drink!"

"I know, sweetie, which is why you need to have a glass of wine." She places a wine glass in front of me and starts opening a bottle.

"Gran, that makes no sense."

"It does. This is your first party, and there will be lots of people drinking. And I think you need to warm up, and see what it's all about while you're in a safe place with someone who loves you."

I bury my face in my hands and groan. If I was a blusher, I'd be scarlet. I glance up at Ryan, who is barely containing his amusement. "I'd tell you she's not normally like this, but I'd be lying. And yes, I saw you looking at the centerpiece on our coffee table. It is indeed a bong." I roll my eyes at him and he stifles a snort.

"Here you go, dear." Gran pours me a large glass. "Dig in!"

Maybe if I enthusiastically fill my plate with food, Gran won't notice that I haven't touched the wine.

But nothing escapes Gran. She reaches over and taps the glass. "Pepper, give that wine a try. Goes great with this meal. You'll love it."

I roll my eyes again. "Don't you go rollin' them eyes at me, girl. If you don't like it, I've got a whole liquor cabinet we can work with."

I take a tentative sip. It's a bit sour and I make a yucky face. "Nope. Don't like it."

"No problem!" Gran claps her hands and stands up. "It's an acquired taste. I was kinda hoping you wouldn't like it." She heads over to the liquor cabinet and pulls down two shot glasses. She pours some vodka into each glass, spoons out some sugar, and then heads to the kitchen.

"Gran?" I call.

"Baby girl, you don't know how long I've been waiting to do this!" She sounds like a kid on Christmas morning.

"I'm so sorry," I say to Ryan. "But I did warn you."

"Pepper, this is more fun than any family dinner I've ever been to. Your Gran's awesome. Seriously." He's given up and is just grinning like an idiot now.

Gran shuffles back over to the liquor cabinet with a lemon in hand and I can't help my adoring smile. "She kind of is, isn't she?"

"You should take the shot with her. I'll make sure nothing happens to you tonight. If you decide to keep drinking or anything," he adds.

"What do you mean? What would happen to me?"

Ryan shrugs. Gran carries the two shot glasses over to the table. She looks over at Ryan. "Do you drink, dear?"

"Not often. I won't drink tonight, Bunny. I'll keep an eye on Pepper. I'm driving anyway. Does she have a curfew?"

Bunny eyes him. "No, no curfew. What kind of party is this, anyway? Pepper, you're wearing a pair of those high top Converse sneakers that your dad used to wear. Are you going to be playing basketball or something?"

"No, Gran. It's just, I heard the party was at Remy Laroche's house, and he lives up the mountain a ways, so I thought we might be outside hanging out." I look at Ryan, who smiles encouragingly. "I've never been to one of these things, but I hear sometimes there are bonfires and stuff, and I need some shoes on so I'm not tramping around in the woods with sandals or heels or something."

"Heels?" Gran scoffs. "Baby girl, you don't own any heels."

I shrug. "I know. I'm just saying, if I did."

"I suppose this is dressed up for you," Gran concedes. She gestures to me and looks at Ryan. "She looks nice, don't you think?" I'm wearing a cutoff jean skirt, and a button-down plaid cowboy-style shirt that I got at a thrift store.

"She always looks great, Bunny," Ryan assures her. "And especially beautiful tonight." He grins at me.

I narrow my eyes at him. "Okay! Shots?" I pick mine up and look at Gran. Her eyes twinkle. We clink glasses and I throw mine back, like I've seen on TV. I'm surprised when it's sweet, and I barely taste the alcohol. It's like lemonade.

"That was actually pretty yummy, Gran!" I exclaim.

"Yup. Now, just cause you can't taste it real strong and it's yummy, don't mean you should keep on drinking. One of those will make you feel good, but more than that and you'll start to get drunk. So no more lemon drops for you tonight."

We finish up dinner and Gran hugs us good-bye. Ryan tries to insist on doing the dishes, but we're shooed out the door.

We wind halfway up Mt. Lincoln before we see the cars parked along the road and hear the music coming from Remy's house. My palms are sweaty and my knee won't stop bouncing. I'm glad Gran gave me that shot. I'm a wreck as it is and I think I'd be freaking out even more without it. Ryan opens my door and I realize I'm still sitting in the passenger seat, twisting my hands. I'm grateful when he takes one and holds it as we walk towards the music. His hand is warm and firm.

If I'm honest with myself, I'm not just nervous about the party, or how people will react to me being here. I'm nervous because I know Jace will be here, and I don't know how he will react. Ryan squeezes my hand and I smile at him.

Remy and Ben are standing outside smoking cigarettes. They're the captains of the soccer team, and I'm surprised to see them smoking. But I try to pretend like I'm not. "Hey, guys." I wave at them stupidly.

Remy puts out his cigarette and walks towards me. "Pepper? What are you doing here? Is everything okay?" He looks concerned.

"What do you mean? Why wouldn't it be okay?" I clutch Ryan's hand. Maybe Remy will make me leave. Oh no. I shouldn't have come.

"Jace isn't here. He doesn't come around our parties as much these days," Ben explains, standing next to me now and staring at my hand locked with Ryan's.

"Oh. Okay. Um. . . why not?" I feel like that's what I'm supposed to ask.

"College parties are more his thing," Remy says, as if that should explain it. I feel like I should know this. Jace is my friend. But he never talks about parties with me.

"That's okay. I'm not here to see Jace. I came with Ryan. Is that okay?" I feel like they are blocking our entrance and that I need to ask permission to enter.

Remy looks at Ben, who shrugs. Remy glances at Ryan and hesitates before relenting. "Sure, yeah, head on in. Keg's out back. I'm trying to keep people outside so the house doesn't get trashed."

As we make our way around the back of the house, Ryan asks me, "What was that all about? Is there something going on with you and Jace? I don't want to piss anyone off bringing you here."

I shake my head. "Honestly, I have no idea why they were being so weird. They're Jace's friends. I don't know them too well."

"I wouldn't worry about it, then," Ryan says reassuringly. "It's your first party so I bet they were just surprised to see you. Everyone will be happy you came."

I recognize the Barbies, a few guys from the football and soccer teams, and a handful of other faces. But there are a lot of people I don't know. Where did they come from?

"Hey, I'm going to grab a water or a soda or something. Do you want anything to drink?" Ryan looks at me. "It doesn't have to be alcohol."

"I don't know. I guess I should have a beer?" I wonder out loud.

"Sure. I'll get you one from the keg. If you don't like it, you can just pass it to someone else."

I look around the crowded yard while Ryan gets our drinks. A few people stumble about drunk, and a couple makes out on a hammock on the back porch. There's a campfire a ways off in the woods, and it looks like a big crowd is gathered around it.

I am both disappointed and relieved that Jace isn't here. It's upsetting that he has a whole life - going to college parties, and doing who-knows-what – that he's never mentioned to me. But I'm relieved that I don't have to face his reaction. He might have made me go home, which would have been totally humiliating. If he ignored me, it'd be even worse. I've always suspected he's too embarrassed of me to bring me around his friends, and it would kill me to have my suspicion confirmed.

I gulp when I see Kayla and Andrea approaching me. Kayla saunters up next to me, a smug expression on her face. "Hey, look who finally decided to join the fun." She bops her hip next to mine like we're old friends, which we're definitely not

"Did you bring Jace with you, Pepper?" Andrea asks as she takes a sip from a wine cooler.

"Um, no. I came with Ryan." I nod in his direction. He looks up and smiles at us, raising a cup of something.

"That's too bad," Kayla coos. "Jace didn't come around much this summer. Always at some UC party, and only graced us with his presence now and then. Maybe he'll show up more now that you're coming out."

"Er. . . doubt it."

Andrea giggles. "You really are clueless, Pepper Jones. I kind of like it."

Ryan saves me when he joins us and hands me a beer. "Do you want to head over to the fire?" he asks.

"Yes!" I exclaim, a little too eager to get away from the Barbies.

Ryan wraps his arm around my waist and I grin into my cup. I don't care what we're calling this, but it's definitely a date. He guides me into the woods, where at least thirty people are gathered. A few couples are cuddled up, and a group of rowdy boys are standing by a table, watching people throw ping pong balls into cups.

I see Dana Foster and Tina Anderson talking with a group of people I can only categorize as the junior class Barbies. They tried to get me to go to parties with them freshman year, when I was still (sort of) friends with them. I knew they only wanted to hang out with me because they thought I'd help them get closer to Jace and his crowd. I was relieved when Zoe befriended me and I became friends with people on the running team instead.

Ryan gestures to a log. "Want to sit?"

I sit on the ground and lean my back against the log. "Here, do you want to lean on me?" Ryan sits with his legs slightly parted and his knees up. I hesitate before leaning back against his shins.

We sit and watch the fire for a few minutes and I try a couple sips of beer. It doesn't taste very good.

Lisa Delany is talking with Connor Locke, Jace's co-captain on the football team, and Dorothy and some of her friends are trying to join the conversation. I try to ignore the glances Lisa and Dorothy keep throwing in my direction.

Ryan runs his fingers up and down my arm. He leans forward to my ear and asks quietly, "Is this okay?" I lean my head back and smile at him.

"Yes. Thank you for bringing me."

The quiet moment is broken when I hear Jace in the woods. "Where is she?" he asks, seemingly to no one in particular.

I stiffen, and Ryan stops moving his finger along my arm. Jace Wilder frightens people. I've never really understood it. Maybe it's because I've known him since he was four years old and I can remember when he carried his stuffed giraffe, Jerry, everywhere with him, but he's never frightened me.

When Jace bursts into the clearing across the campfire, green eyes blazing, I think I can actually see what frightens people. He looks volatile.

"Jace?" I sit up and I hate that my voice quivers.

I can see Jace's chest rising and falling as he breathes deeply. His hands clench and unclench. It feels like minutes, although I know it's only seconds, before he slowly makes his way around the campfire and crouches in front of me. "Jace, are you on drugs? You're scaring me."

His muscles around his shoulders tense and then relax. "No, Pepper, I don't do drugs."

"I wouldn't know. There's a lot about you I don't know." I don't mean to sound accusing, but I can't help my anger. He doesn't even party with the high school kids anymore? I should have known this.

He should have told me. I have no idea who his new college friends are.

Jace sighs. He takes the beer from my hand and places it on the ground. "Does Bunny know you're here?"

"Of course. We did shots together before we left. Ryan came for dinner. She's thrilled I'm going to a party." I feel Ryan's legs stiffen behind me. He hasn't said anything.

"Are you drunk?" Jace asks. He still hasn't looked at Ryan.

"Of course not," I scoff. "Not that it's your business."

Jace's jaw clenches. "Do you want me to take you home?" His green eyes are so intent, I feel like he could break glass with that gaze. But I won't give in.

"Do you want me to leave that badly? Get over it, Jace. I'm not doing anything to embarrass you. I'm just sitting here. Ryan will take me home when I'm ready. You can go back to your college party, or wherever you were. You smell like chlorine." I lean back against Ryan's shins, pick up my drink, and look at the fire, avoiding Jace's penetrating gaze. I take a sip of beer, defiantly. I know I'm acting like a child, and I hate that he's making me feel this way. But seriously, what's the big deal?

Jace runs his hand through his messy fauxhawk. He stands up and watches the fire, but doesn't move. After a moment, he stalks off towards the table where people are playing beer pong. I turn back to Ryan. "Sorry about that."

Ryan frowns. "There's nothing to apologize for, Pepper. Although I can't say I understand what just happened."

"That makes two of us. Jace is just... intense. He likes things a certain way. I think he likes to keep his friendship with me separate from the rest of his social life." I squirm slightly. "It's kind of hurtful, to be honest. He doesn't like me being here."

"I caught that. It looks like he's staying," Ryan says, nodding toward where Jace is leaning against a tree.

People quickly start gathering around him. He's wearing swim trunks and a sleeveless shirt that shows off his chest and arms. His presence dominates the clearing, and it's not just his six foot three inch height. People are drawn to him. Connor pats him on the shoulder, says something in his ear, and steps back, punching him lightly on the arm. Andrea and Kayla approach him and hand him a drink. Kayla brushes her hand along his chest and giggles at something Connor says.

"Yeah. Hopefully he'll ignore me." I turn myself around and sit cross-legged facing toward Ryan and away from Jace. "So, tell me about California. I know you stayed there last year even though your family moved here. We all heard about your dad as the coach at UC, and I read that article about you in *Running Fast*."

He laughs. "Yeah, that was weird. Seeing myself on the cover of magazines in grocery stores was really unnerving." He places a hand loosely on my knee and moves his thumb in small circles. "At first, I was going to finish up high school in California. I liked my coach, my teammates. I didn't want to leave the friends I've had my whole life. My uncle and his family live in the same town and they were happy to have me. Actually, I had a girlfriend and that probably had something to do with it too." He smiles sheepishly at me.

"But you didn't end up staying for your senior year. You're here instead."

Ryan shrugs. "Yeah. Most of my friends were seniors last year, and they graduated. Plus my parents and my little brother were pushing for me to come out here. They said I'd really like it. Now, I can see if I do. I can go to UC if I want, and if I don't like it here, I can always go to college somewhere else."

"And the girlfriend?" I look down at my drink and take a quick sip.

"It's okay," he reassures me. "We are on a kind of, not really, date. You can ask. She was my girlfriend for almost three years. Started going out when I was a freshman. She was a year ahead of me, which is partly why most of my friends were a grade ahead, too. I was really into it at first. I thought it was so cool an older girl liked me. But eventually I started to lose interest." He shrugs. "I didn't want to break it off, since it would make everything weird with our group of friends. It was easier to just stay together. But we ended it at the beginning of the summer, when she graduated."

I don't really know what to say. I'm sorry? Do you miss her? Are you looking for a replacement? So I just take another sip of my beer.

"She wasn't a runner," Ryan adds. "And running is such a huge part of my life, of who I am. I think that was part of why I wasn't really into it anymore. She didn't really get it. It wasn't her fault, but she didn't understand competitive sports. She liked to watch and cheer, but the training, the excitement of racing, all that, I couldn't share it with her." Ryan looks right at me when he says this.

I swallow. I understand what he means. That's one of the reasons I became friends with Zoe and Charlie instead of Tina and Dana. "Yeah, I get that." Before I can say anything else, Ryan looks behind me and his face stiffens.

"Jace?" I ask, without turning to look.

"Yeah. He's glaring." Ryan sighs. "Let's get up. Do you want to play beer pong?"

"I don't know. Will I have to drink a lot?"

Ryan laughs as he grabs my hands to help me up. "Probably. It depends on if you're good or not. If you're winning, you'll drink less. But we can put a tiny bit of beer in the cups, just in case."

We wander over to the table, where a couple stands on each end. They look familiar, but I don't think they go to our school. "You guys want winner?" one of the guys in a white polo shirt asks us.

"Sure, if no one else has called it," Ryan tells him.

"It's all you, man. We nearly got these guys finished off." He shoots the ping pong ball and sinks it in the last cup.

The other guy, who's also wearing a polo shirt, nods at Ryan. "Hey man, I don't think we've met. I'm Pierce."

"Ryan. And this is Pepper." Ryan puts an arm around me.

"Yeah, I know. Pepper Jones," Pierce says. The girl next to him darts her eyes in my direction. She runs her eyes up and down my body, like she's checking me out.

"Sorry. I, um, don't know if we've met?" I ask Pierce, feeling bad already in case I don't remember him and I should.

"No, but you know, you were in the newspaper a couple times for running," Pierce explains quickly.

The girl puts out her hand to me. "I'm Emma." We shake hands.

"Are we going to play or what?" white polo shirt guy calls.

Ryan guides me over to our side of the table. He sets up the cups in a triangle and pours a sip of beer in each one. I notice that white polo shirt guy is pouring half a can in each of the cups on his end of the table.

The girl on the other side has long, straight blonde hair and huge glossy lips. She's wearing a pink frilly blouse and white jean shorts.

This girl could be the inspiration for Zoe's label. She practically has a sign on her forehead saying "Barbie." The couple introduces themselves as Forbes and Serena.

Pierce and Emma stay to watch. The four of them are seniors at Lincoln Academy. Forbes and Pierce are on the football team. I'm surprised they're at this party. I always thought the rivalry between the schools kept the social circles from overlapping. I guess I'm really out of the loop.

Ryan and I are a good team, probably because we're sober and Forbes and Serena are not. We take them out pretty quickly, and I barely have to drink any beer. I cringe when I hear Jace call next game.

He watches me while he arranges the cups in a triangle, and I try to ignore him. Madeline saunters up next to him; her long wavy brown hair is moving in the slight breeze. She squeezes his bicep and places her cleavage in Jace's line of sight. "Need a partner?" Her voice is husky and seductive and it makes me want to puke.

"Hi, Madeline," Jace says smoothly. He tucks her under his shoulder for a hug. Madeline's the queen bee (or, as Zoe likes to say, B for bitch) at Lincoln Academy.

Madeline turns to face me with a satisfied smirk. I notice her hand around Jace's waist ventures down around to the waistband of his swim trunks, and she skims her fingers back and forth. "Nice to see you out, Pepper," she says sweetly.

"You too," I say dully. "This is Ryan," I add as I lean next to his shoulder, taking comfort in his presence while being forced to witness the display in front of us.

I don't play as well this round. I'm far too distracted by Madeline's hands all over Jace, and his acceptance of her touches. I notice him staring at her ass and cleavage more than once, and I'm ready to leave. I've probably had about two beers in addition to the shot with Gran at this point. I'm feeling more emotional than I should.

I've seen girls all over Jace before, so it must be the drinks that are getting me fired up. Plus Madeline is simply gorgeous. In purple shorts that hug her hips, and a silky white tank top that makes her boobs look humongous, she somehow pulls off a glamorous look while playing beer pong around a campfire. After we lose the game, I tell Ryan I'm ready to head home.

I don't say goodbye to Jace and I don't look at him as we leave. On our way up the path, I nearly trip when I recognize Wesley walking towards me. He and Jace had some sort of falling out when they started high school, and Wes stopped hanging out with me, too. I've only seen him a few times around town over the past three years.

Like Jace, Wes is wearing swim trunks, and when he approaches, I smell chlorine. He's as good-looking as I remember, with his ruffled blonde hair and blue eyes. "Pepper?" He squints at me. "Is that you?"

"Yeah, hey Wesley." I give him a brief hug. "This is Ryan, he's new at Brockton, and on the cross team with me."

The guys shake hands. "Wes used to go to school with us until high school. He's at Lincoln Academy now." I hear Wes is kind of like the Jace of his school, except his "big fish" status is in a much smaller pond.

"So, is Jace here? He took off without saying anything from the party we were at earlier."

"Huh? I thought you guys hated each other. I didn't know you were hanging out again." One more thing I didn't know. Last I heard they were rivals, not friends. "Jace never tells me anything. What's his problem?"

"Don't worry about it, Pep. It's not like we're good friends again. We just sort of have an understanding. We can hang at the same parties without shit going down. It's a mutually beneficial alliance," Wes explains.

"You make it sound like a business deal," I say sassily and put my hands on my hips for added effect. Okay, so I'm feeling the alcohol a little bit, and I have an attitude right now.

Wes opens his mouth to respond, but we're interrupted by Jace, who not-so-subtly puts his arm around me and pulls me away from Ryan and Wes. I shove him away and take Ryan's hand. I'm pissed. I feel like I know nothing of Jace's life anymore. "I'll see you later, Wes. Come on Ryan, let's get out of here."

"Hang on," Jace says calmly. He puts his hand on Ryan's shoulder and nods at Wes, who pulls me towards him. Jace starts talking to Ryan in a low voice, and I can't hear what he's saying.

I start to ask Wes what the heck is going on, but the conversation between Jace and Ryan is over before it started. Ryan takes my hand again and we walk back up the path. "You want to tell me what that was about?" I ask.

"Jace just checked to make sure I was sober to drive, and to make sure you got home safe," Ryan says casually. He probably said something else, but Ryan doesn't seem intent on sharing.

When we pull up outside my apartment, I turn to Ryan. "Hey," I say softly. "I had a really good time tonight with you." I feel like I should apologize for Jace's behavior, but I already apologized once. There's no point in bringing it up again. Besides, it's not my fault Jace was acting like jerk.

Ryan takes my hand and rubs his thumb against mine. "I had a really good time tonight too, Pepper." He swallows, and I wonder if he's going to kiss me. "Come on, I'll walk you to your door."

Music is playing from one of the other apartments in our building, and a couple of drunken girls stumble out. "A lot of college kids live here," I explain. "Gran has been known to crash a party or two."

"And by crash, I assume you mean she joins the fun, and doesn't tell them to quiet down?" he asks as we reach the door.

I turn to face him. "Exactly." I pause, giving him an opportunity to kiss me before I go inside. I *want* him to kiss me. But he hesitates, and I'm not sure what to do. "Thanks for taking me tonight," I say lamely.

"Thanks for coming." Ryan places his hands on my hips before I can open my door. He leans down and brushes his lips tentatively against mine. I move closer, encouraging him to deepen the kiss. He understands what I'm communicating and his lips part just enough to slip his tongue into my mouth. Ryan's hands hold my hips firmly, but he doesn't pull me into his body. My hands rest on his chest as his lips slowly caress mine. The warmth of his hands and lips spread to my core, and I gasp a little at the unfamiliar sensation. I start to tug his tee shirt, wanting to feel his body pressed to mine. Instead, Ryan pulls back, breathing heavily.

We watch each other, regaining our composure. I'm alarmed by my reaction. "Whoa," I breathe out.

"Yeah." He nods slowly in response, taking calming breaths. "I should drive home now."

"Okay." I nod in agreement, dazed.

He takes my hand and squeezes it. "Goodnight, Pepper."

Chapter 7

"Did you see this month's *Running Fast Magazine*?" Claire asks me and Zoe on Sunday morning.

The three of us are standing in warrior pose in my living room. The furniture is pushed to the side to make room for our yoga session.

"Yeah, but I've never heard of any of those girls that they picked as top contenders," I respond. "Have you?"

"I have!" Zoe pipes up. "You can totally kick those girls' butts."

"How would you know?" I ask her. "They're all from different states. I've never raced any of them."

"Oh, I check out the results and stuff online, and the discussion forums," Zoe explains.

"I like your confidence in me, Zoe, but cross isn't like track. You can't just look up our times and compare them because the course is different every time, even if the distance is the same." Pretty much all high school cross country courses are five kilometers, or three point one miles, but the terrain varies from flat and sandy to hills with rocks.

We move into sun worship pose, pause for a breath, and then lower into downward dog pose. I relish the feeling of a full body stretch as I arch my back.

"Yeah, but you won State last year. They should have picked you," Claire says, sounding offended on my behalf.

"Claire, there are fifty states. They can't pick all the State winners," I point out. The blood starts to drain to my head – probably from the pose, but possibly from the conversation as well.

"The discussion forums think you're a top contender, Pepper," Zoe says, her voice muffled as she moves into child's pose.

I copy her, letting my body rest. I really wanted to run this morning with Dave, but Coach insists I take one day off a week for injury prevention.

"I just want to qualify, guys. I think I should focus on that for now, and not what place I'm going to get."

We rest quietly for a few minutes, lost in our thoughts as we listen to the soothing yoga music.

I like being an unknown on the national scene. It's hard enough having expectations at the state level. My teammates, Coach, people at school, folks around town, and even Jace, are all aware of my potential now that I've had some success.

I'm pretty sure that we'll make it to State this year as a team. Last year, we just barely missed making it by one place, and Zoe was sick with a cold, Dorothy was hungover, and we really didn't have any other strong runners. So far this year, Claire and Zoe raced great at our first meet, and Jenny is an awesome addition to the team. Dorothy fills out the top five, and isn't as reliable, but with four strong girls we can count on, the odds are in our favor.

But if we do make it to State, that's when the heat will really turn up. Though none of us have said it yet, there's a chance Brockton Public could win the State championship for the first time in fifteen years. And they *won't* have a chance if I get injured or have a bad race. I don't want to let anyone down.

The yoga CD ends and switches to a familiar dance mix. Gran pops her head in the living room. "I love this song!" she exclaims as she dances her way towards us, swinging her hips to Mariah Carrey.

Zoe and I glance at each other and grin. Claire shakes her head and announces she has to get home to study. She knows what's about to go down.

Zoe, Gran and I choreographed some rocking moves to every song on this dance mix. We immediately move into position and belt the lyrics as we shake our booties, roll our hips, and twirl around in a synchronized effort. Gran hikes up her sweat pants and pushes her wiry hair back with a head band. Zoe and I lose our tee shirts as we work up a sweat.

Several songs later, after a dramatic rendition of *Beautiful Life* by Ace of Base, I turn towards the kitchen to get something to drink. Jace is leaning against the doorframe with his arms crossed and a huge smile on his face. His green eyes are dancing with amusement.

My heart jumps into my throat. I spent the last thirty minutes prancing around, and I cringe thinking of my shameless Beyoncé wannabe performance. Yeah, that "dance like there's no one watching" proverb? I can totally rock that. Except this time, I had an unknown audience. If there was any hope Jace might start looking at me like a mature, attractive young woman, I've blown it.

"How long have you been standing there?" I blow a loose lock of hair from my forehead.

He shrugs and grins wider. He's wearing a tee shirt with the sleeves cut off and my eyes are drawn to his biceps. They look impossibly large with his arms folded like that.

I shake my head and push past him towards the kitchen. Someone turns the music down, and I hear Zoe squeak an embarrassed "hello" to Jace.

I chug a cold glass of lemonade. It helps to cool down my body temperature, but my heart is still racing. Zoe mumbles something about needing to pick up her little brothers, and waves good-bye. It cracks me up how flustered she gets around Jace. But she's just like any girl, after all.

"Boy, this old lady needs a shower after that energizing workout!" Gran huffs. She shuffles off to her bedroom.

I glance at Jace, who is still leaning against the doorframe, watching me. I swear, his jet-black hair is always perfectly messed up in a wavy, tousled fauxhawk that begs for girls to run their fingers through it. And why do his cheekbones have to be chiseled like a sculpture? It's so irritating.

I stomp off to my room. I grab a clean tee shirt from my dresser and pull it on over my sports bra. Jace follows me inside and shuts the door. He sits on the edge of my bed, and I know he wants to talk to me about something.

I sit down on the bed facing him, but as far away as possible. Still not enough distance. It seems like the more emotional I am – even if it's embarrassment I'm feeling – the crazier my hormones get. I don't trust myself with Jace in my bedroom right now.

"So what's up?" I ask.

He runs his hand through his hair. "Do you really like this Ryan guy?" he asks.

"That's not what I expected. I thought you were going to be doing some explaining, not asking me questions." I fold my arms across my chest.

"What do you want me to explain?" Jace leans back against my pillow and rests his hands behind his head. He must be completely oblivious about how his position makes me feel. I'm having difficulty concentrating.

"For starters, why were you angry that I was at that party last night?"

He brings his hands around to his lap and straightens his shoulders. "I was angry. You're right. It's just, that party was pretty low key, but parties can get out of hand. Cops show up. People fight. Drugs. Guys. We live in a college town, Pep, and high school parties can quickly turn into college parties, and I just worry about you in those situations." He glances at my confused expression. "I know you're a smart girl, Pep, and I know you won't do anything stupid. But I don't trust other people. Even girls can be pretty vicious, and I don't want you to get pulled into that scene. I don't want you to get hurt."

"So it's not because you're embarrassed of me?" I mutter stupidly.

Jace sits up and rubs my back. "Pep, of course not. That's probably one of the stupidest things I've heard you say. Why would you even think that?" He pulls me in for a hug.

I mumble into his chest, "I don't know."

Jace pulls away before I can get too comfortable, but leaves his hands on my shoulders. "Let me get this right," I say. "You don't like me hanging out with your friends or going to parties because you're worried something might happen to me?"

"Yes, Pepper. I care about you. So much," Jace tells me. "You know this."

I do. I care about him too. Just in a different way.

"So, you're protective?" I ask. He nods once. I force myself to ask the next question. "Like a big brother?"

He hesitates, and my heart squeezes in my chest. Please don't say yes. Please *please* let what I heard in the locker room be a misunderstanding.

"Yeah, I guess you could say that," he says quietly.

I can't breathe for a second, and I realize I was holding my breath.

"I don't really know what it's like to be a big brother, but I know I don't think of you like other girls."

Knowing how Jace thinks about other girls, this is not good news for me. I suddenly feel like I might throw up the coffee cake I ate for breakfast.

"How do you feel about Ryan? You didn't tell me you were going out with him." His green eyes darken in disapproval.

"I like him, Jace. We had a nice time last night. Why, do you not like him? It seems like you don't."

Jace sighs. "It's not that. He seems like a good guy, really. Not good enough for you, but no one is, in my opinion."

I roll my eyes. "Will you stop being angry if I go out with him again?" I need to move on. Date other people. Let go of any hidden hopes I harbored for Jace and me. I didn't know I was still holding onto them until now. Until he told me to my face he feels like a big brother towards me.

Jace puts his hands on his thighs and rubs them back and forth. I want to reach out and put my hands on his. But I can't think like that anymore. Besides, how can I be thinking like that when we're talking about me dating someone else? I mentally slap myself.

"So, you want to keep going out with this guy?" Jace turns to me again, searching my eyes.

"Yes," I tell him.

"Okay. Just, be careful." He grins sheepishly at me. "I know you will be. But, you know. I don't know. I'm going to shut up." Jace stands and stretches.

The conversation is too heavy. I don't have the energy to ask about his college friends, or his friendship with Wesley Jamison. I just want to curl up in a ball on my bed and feel sorry for myself for being head over heels about a guy like Jace Wilder.

"You okay, Pep?"

I smile weakly. "Yeah. I'm good."

"You know you can call me any time about Ryan, if you're with him and need me to pick you up, or you're upset. Anything." He takes my hands and pulls me up from the bed.

"I know." We make our way to the kitchen. "I gotta get back to homework. Want some coffee cake for the road?"

"No thanks." He kisses me on the head, like he did the other day in the cafeteria, and heads out. Platonic. It's now my least favorite word.

★ ★ ★

I mope around for a few minutes after Jace leaves, but what I really want to do is go for a long run in the foothills. I need to get out of the house and clear my head.

I try to distract myself with homework, and when that doesn't work, I Google the girls listed as the top contenders in *Running Fast Magazine.* There's a lengthy interview with Jessica Lillis, who placed second last year, and is predicted to win this year. She's a senior at a high school in upstate New York.

In the interview, Jessica explains a typical week of training, and I'm blown away when she says that she typically runs twice as many miles a week as I do. I read some of the comments on the article, and realize that her training is fairly typical for a national-level high school runner. When I click on links to different discussion forums about high school running, I'm shocked to see my name appear in several threads.

Most of the comments are flattering, and predict that I will break into the national scene this year. But what happens when I have a bad race? What will they say if I don't live up to their expectations?

Before I know it, I'm lacing up my trail runners and changing into running shorts. Dave hops off the couch, tugs his leash off its hook and wags his tail by the door.

As soon as we hit the trails, I feel better. The hollow feeling Jace left me with is still there, but my spirits lift with the familiar rhythm of my feet on dirt. A soft breeze ruffles the leaves in the trees, and Dave lifts his snout in appreciation of the sweet fresh air.

Though my head has always known Jace would never be mine, I think my heart has been holding onto the possibility. But it's time to let go, and move on.

I'm excited about how good things feel between Ryan and me. That kiss... it felt more than good. It meant something. I know it did.

My legs feel strong today, nice and loose after yoga. I know I should take the shorter loop, but my legs float along effortlessly and I simply don't want the run to end. I take the long loop that winds up a mountain, the sound of Dave's panting and my steady breathing the only noises along the way. At the top, I climb up a boulder and take in the view of Brockton below.

My body tingles from exertion, but my head is calm, and my heart -- well, it hurts, but maybe now it can start healing.

Chapter 8

"Hey Coach," I greet Tom at the beginning of practice the next day.

"Pepper, how are you?"

"I'm feeling good," I tell him honestly. He always checks in to see if anything hurts, or if I'm getting tired. "But I couldn't help myself, and I kind of went for a long run yesterday. I know I wasn't supposed to, but I really wanted to."

Coach smiles. "You don't have to look so guilty about it."

"But," I start to say, but he cuts me off.

"Yes, one day off from running each week is important, but it's great that you love running so much." He smiles at me. "I don't want that to change. It's okay to be flexible with the training plan. The general idea is to make sure you get some recovery days in between long runs and workouts, and that you don't start racing hard until the end of the season. So why don't you take today off, instead?"

"But then I'll miss practice. I never miss practice. I'm the captain, and it doesn't seem right that –"

"Pepper, take today off," he says firmly. "You can stick around and do some strength exercises if you want, but you don't need to. How long did you run for yesterday?"

I think for a second. "I didn't bring a watch, but that loop usually takes about an hour and a half."

"I might modify tomorrow's workout for you then, as well. Maybe have you do the hill workout with the girls instead of the boys."

I hate missing practice, and I'm not sure how I feel about a "flexible" training plan. Today's practice is just an easy running day, so it's not a huge deal to miss, but modifying tomorrow's hill workout? I don't like it.

I do some homework while I wait for Ryan to finish practice. I haven't spoken to him since Saturday night, and I'm eager to see him. How will he act? Are we more than friends now? Do I want that?

I quickly realize the answer must be yes, I do, because why else would I be so bummed out when he acts exactly the same towards me, as though the kiss never happened? On the way home, he's attentive and friendly, but he doesn't touch me, or express an interest in hanging out together again.

I shake it off and talk to him more about Coach's training philosophy. "I guess I feel like he's holding me back," I complain. "I've never been injured and I've never felt burnt out or over-trained before. So what's the big deal if I run more? It should only make me stronger, right?"

Ryan smiles. "I totally get where you're coming from, Pepper. But did you think that you've never been injured *because* Coach Tom knows what he's doing? Moderate training is counterintuitive, in some ways, but what's the point in training your ass off only to get injured?" He shrugs with both hands on the wheel. "Once your body gets tired, running isn't much fun."

"But I'm *not* tired, that's what I'm saying." I know I'm being whiney, but it's really bugging me.

"Injury and fatigue happen fast, and then there's not much you can do about it." He glances at me before continuing. "My dad reviews a ton of high school programs and sees how runners from different programs do in college and after. The ones who do the best long-term are usually the ones who don't do crazy intense training in high school."

I sigh heavily. I know I should trust Coach, especially if the reigning national champion agrees with his approach, but holding back is not in my nature.

"Look," Ryan continues, "a lot of runners need to be pushed just to show up to practice, let alone run hard. But for someone like you, who really loves it, Coach's job is just to keep you healthy. There's no doubt, with your talent, that you'll get stronger and faster."

"You sound so wise, it's hard not to listen to you," I say grumpily.

Ryan laughs. "I just hear about this stuff all the time with my dad as a coach. I'm happy that I have the opportunity to help you out. I really want to go to Nationals together, Pepper."

He smiles at me as we pull up outside my apartment building. With a dimple on each cheek, and those bright blue eyes, Ryan has the all-American boy good looks.

"You want to stay for dinner? Gran always makes plenty." And Jace doesn't come by as much these days, I think.

He considers for a moment, and then says, "I should get home. My Mom's expecting me. Thanks though."

"Okay, see you tomorrow then."

He must have decided he didn't want to pursue anything with me after all. Maybe I'm a bad kisser.

When the entire week goes by and Ryan shows no interest in taking things further than friendship, I'm slightly shocked by my devastation. I guess I really did like him. I've lost my usual appetite, and I'm constantly grumpy.

I want to run harder and longer to get out my negative feelings, but I'm trying hard to be patient. I run with the girls for the hill workout on Tuesday, and Coach keeps yelling at me to slow down. I get to run with the boys again for the speed workout on Thursday, and I hammer out the half-mile repeats. It helps me work out some of my negative energy, but I'm still in a funk and I can't figure out how to break it.

* * *

When Zoe organizes tubing on Saturday after our long run, I eagerly agree to go. It's time to stop wallowing and have fun.

I wear my white bikini with purple polka dots. We meet the group at the park where most people start the tubing down Wolf Creek. Charlie and Zoe drive down to the end of the creek to drop off Zoe's mom's minivan so we have a ride back up at the end.

I'm surprised to see Ryan leaning against his car in the parking lot when we all meet. I know he eats at the table with Jace's crowd on Mondays, Wednesdays and Fridays, when he has a different lunch period than me, and everyone's heard that Lisa has made her intentions to get with him very clear. Ryan's definitely been accepted into the senior inner circle, the people who the gossip revolves around, and one of the hottest girls in school wants to date him. I didn't think he'd spend his Saturday afternoon hanging out with the team.

Zoe squeals when she rejoins us. "Check it out! Check it out!" She shows us a bottle of Captain Morgan peeking out from under her towel. "I hope you all brought water bottles! Claire, stop looking at me like that! It's still early in the season, and I think we all deserve a little fun." She wiggles her eyebrows.

Charlie raises his hand. "I brought the mixer."

"Charlie!" I exclaim. "Since when do you drink?!"

He shrugs sheepishly. "I don't, really. But I'm a senior in high school. I figure I should go to college with at least a little experience under my belt."

Claire and Ryan volunteer to be our designated drivers. Zoe starts filling up people's water bottles with rum and Coke. I tell her to just put a tiny bit of rum in mine. I don't think I'm going to like the stuff, but I feel comfortable drinking a little with this group.

While we unload the tubes from Charlie's truck, I see Jace's Jeep on the other side of the parking lot. He's leaning against the passenger side door, and a petite brunette is plastered against him. She's wearing nothing but a bright red string bikini, and Jace's hands are squeezing her butt. Her hands are between them while they make out and I quickly look away, but not before seeing exactly where her hands are.

"Hey Zoe," I call over to her. "Can you add more rum to mine?" She grins and dumps in more.

I've never seen Jace with another girl like this. I've seen girls flirt with him and seek his attention, but I rarely see him give more than a polite or indulgent response. Logically, I know he's been intimate with lots of girls. But I really don't like witnessing it. I take a sip from the water bottle and grimace.

Ryan, who I didn't even notice was standing next to me, laughs softly. "Take it easy on that, Pepper."

I'm not happy with him either. I take my inner tube from Charlie and stomp off towards the creek, taking small sips along the way. A group of guys and girls, whom I don't recognize and look to be UC students, are lounging by the creek entrance, smoking cigarettes. I sit on my inner tube in the shallow water, waiting for my friends to catch up before I start down the river.

I watch the college kids. Most of them have tattoos, and some of the guys have silver or gold chain necklaces. The guys look tough, and the girls hard. I take another sip from my water bottle.

"Oh, there you are!" I hear a girl's voice call out from the path. I turn to see if it's one of my friends. It's not. It's the girl who was with Jace; they're holding hands. I've never seen her before today.

She has a tattoo peeking out from the bottom of her bathing suit, and I just bet Jace has seen the rest of it. "We were up in the parking lot waiting for you. We didn't know we were meeting down here."

"No problem," one of the guys says. He puts out his cigarette and does a little handshake thing with Jace.

I shrink into my inner tube, wishing I hadn't come down by myself. I turn away and look out across the river, while continuing to sip my rum and Coke. It's starting to taste sweet now, and I think I'm already feeling tipsy. I'm relieved when I see Jace's group hop on their tubes and push off down the river. No one seems to notice me.

"Pepper?" I look over at Jace when I hear my name but I avert my eyes when I see the girl climb between his legs into the same tube as him. That can't be comfortable. But still, I'm jealous.

"Hey Jace." I try to sound cool and unaffected by the PDA.

"I saw Ryan and Zoe and those guys heading down here. Are you with them?" He steadies his tube but he's already starting to float away.

"Yup. I'm cool!" I call out. I wave and he waves back. I watch him lean down to say something in the girl's ear.

"Pepper! Have you tried your drink? What do you think? I stole it from my parents' liquor cabinet." Zoe bounces towards me, the crew behind her.

"Yeah. It's awesome. Thanks." I stifle a small burp. "I think I might be drunk already though."

"I'll keep an eye on you." Ryan squats down next to my tube. "You know, in case you fall out or something."

"I know how to swim, Ryan. But thank you." I tell everyone to wait a few minutes to let the other group get further ahead of us. I don't want to keep seeing Jace and his college girl.

It doesn't take much before we are all feeling a little crazy from the drinks. Ryan keeps his tube by mine the whole way. I find myself stuck in an eddy at one point and Ryan hops out of his tube to pull me back into the flowing river.

"Ryan?" I ask, feeling bold. "I'm kind of confused. I thought we had a really good time last week. I know it wasn't really a date, but. . . I thought you might ask me on one. Was I wrong to think that? Do you not like me that way?"

Ryan pauses, holding on to both our tubes. The sun glints off his wet chest, and he really does look good leaning over me. Before he can answer, I tell him, "I'd like to kiss you again. Do you want that too?"

"Remy, Ben and Connor talked to me," he says. "They were cool about it. But they told me I should think about backing off from you."

"Huh? Why?"

"They weren't very clear about it, just that Jace is real protective of you, and he has a temper. I guess he's been really angry or something and they're worried he'll lose it if you and I are together."

I nod. Jace does have a temper. "Jace likes to act like a big brother. But don't worry, he said he likes you, and that it's okay if I keep going out with you. I talked to him about it."

"Really?" Ryan looks surprised. "It's not only what the guys said that stopped me from asking you out again, though, Pepper. I really like you, and I wouldn't have let Jace's problems get in the way. It's just, I've seen the way you look at him, Pepper." Ryan looks right at me, and says quietly, "I don't think I can compete with that."

"Oh." I can't deny it. I didn't know that others could see it too. "Is it that obvious?"

"To me? Yeah. I look at you a lot. I can't help it." He laughs. "I probably look at you the same way you look at Jace."

"I'm sorry, Ryan. I really like you. I just... I've always had a crush on Jace. I mean, he's *Jace*. I think every girl has a little bit of a crush on him."

"Maybe." He gets back on his tube. Before pushing off he turns his head around to look at me. "Jace is a hard guy to read, but -- I think he looks at you that way too."

Jace *is* hard to read, and Ryan doesn't know what he's talking about. Ryan adds, "For now, let's keep hanging out, being friends, but maybe wait to decide if we should take it further?"

I consider for a moment before replying. "Yeah, that sounds good. If you won't be my boyfriend, then I want you to at least be my friend."

"That's exactly what I thought. Which is why I didn't want to try anything else and end up not being friends at all if it didn't work out."

"Come on, let's catch up to the group." I push off from a rock and drag his tube with mine.

"They're probably way ahead of us by now," Ryan says.

"I don't know. We're all serious lightweights. I'm pretty sure it's the first time drinking for most of them. I bet they're all stuck on the bank somewhere and haven't even realized it yet." Ryan grabs my foot and swings my tube around so I'm going down backwards. "Hey!" I call out. He laughs and shrugs.

We don't catch up to the group on the river and they're waiting for us when we get to the exit spot. Zoe teases us, implying that we've been up to no good, but I shush her.

Jace's group is nowhere to be seen, and I'm relieved. But when we get up to the parking lot and pile into Zoe's mom's minivan, I see Jace watching me. He's sitting on the bumper of a pick-up truck. The college girl he was with is nowhere to be seen. It's just Jace and the four other guys he went down the river with, standing around. Jace isn't smoking a cigarette, but the rest of them are. I ignore his gaze and hop into the back of the van.

Claire takes the driver's seat. I peek out the window one more time but Jace is no longer looking our way. He turns to get into the passenger seat of the pickup, and the other guys follow. Even amongst his college buddies, he seems to be the leader.

"That's the look I'm talking about," Ryan whispers into my ear. His warm breath on my neck feels comforting, but I know he's right. I was so focused on Jace that I hardly noticed him slide in next to me. It's probably only fair to Ryan to stay just friends for now. But will I ever shake my feeling for Jace Wilder? And what happens if I can't?

Chapter 9

The next Saturday is our only home meet, and the hardest one to sit out. I won this meet last year, and it was the first time I'd ever won a race. I don't know what I'd do if Ryan weren't jogging along the course with me during the race. It's a lot easier to trust Coach's plans with Ryan at my side.

The team looks strong, and I'm happy to see Zoe take first place. It's a hot day, and I'm not great at racing in the heat. Zoe, on the other hand, always has her best races on warm days.

I'm warming down with Zoe on the sidewalk after the race when a BMW pulls up next to us.

"Hey, Pepper!" someone yells from the window.

Zoe and I stop jogging and peer in the car. It's Forbes, the guy from Lincoln Academy that I played beer pong against at Remy's party. I see that Pierce is in the driver's seat, and another guy is in the back.

"Oh, hey guys, how's it going?"

"We're on our way to a game. Did you race already?" Forbes asks.

"I didn't. But Zoe did. She won." I point my thumb in her direction. "Zoe, this is Forbes and Pierce," I introduce them.

"Hi!" Zoe waves and smiles eagerly. She's boy-crazy.

"Cool. Do you girls want to come to a pool party after our scrimmage?" Pierce asks.

Normally I would say no, but I can practically feel the excitement vibrating off of Zoe. I can't let her down. And, since I know they only just met her, I figure I'm the one who is supposed to respond.

"I guess. What time?"

Forbes turns to check with Pierce. "Come on over to Wes's place around three. Or we can pick you up if you need a ride?"

"I can drive!" Zoe volunteers.

Pierce hands Forbes a piece of paper and a pen and Forbes writes something down. "Here's my and Pierce's numbers, so we can give you directions or whatever."

I take it. "Thanks. I think I know where Wes's house is. He still lives in Meadow Ridge, right?" It's one of the fancy gated neighborhoods with killer views, and even though it's been three years, I'm pretty sure I can find it.

"Yup. All right, we gotta get going. See you later!" Pierce says before pulling away from the curb.

I glance at Zoe. When the car is out of sight, she does her trademark happy dance. I laugh, pleased to have a distraction from my fidgety legs that are anxious to race, and the increasing pressure to make Nationals. We continue jogging --well, Zoe is skipping, but I've got a little extra kick too.

When I tell Gran about the party at Wesley's house, she is less enthusiastic than I expected. "I don't know, Pepper. Will Jace be there?"

"Probably not. I mean, they seem to be friends again, but I think it's a Lincoln party. I could be wrong, but still, it's at Wes's house. You know him."

"I *used* to know him. But he could be bad news now for all I know. You haven't had that boy around for years. What about that nice Ryan fella? Will he be there?"

"No, Gran. I told you, it's a Lincoln party. I don't really know who else is coming."

Gran harrumphs and crosses her arms over her chest. "All right. You can go. But you call me if there's any funny business."

"What kind of funny business?" Since when was she concerned about beer or pot? "I mean, I'm guessing there will be drinking. Is that what you mean?"

"I don't know exactly. I don't mean drinking. I expect that. But if you feel at all uncomfortable, you call me and I'll come get ya. I'm drivin' you. I don't want any drinking and driving."

"Gran, you hate driving. Zoe said she'll drive."

"I'm driving," Gran insists.

I let it drop and change the subject. "Oh, Gran? Um. . . I think it might be polite to bring something to drink. Do you have anything I can bring?" I know she knows I mean alcohol, but I can't bring myself to say that specifically.

Gran smiles mischievously at me, her good humor restored after I let her have her way. "I have the perfect thing." Gran puts together a bag with margarita mix, tequila, chips and salsa. "Someone there will know how to mix margaritas, I would think. But the instructions are on the back of the mix if you need it."

I change into a coral bikini with beaded strings and a simple white cotton dress with cap sleeves. It used to be a wardrobe staple but it's too short now. Perfect for a pool party. I knew I'd find another use for it someday.

As we pull into Zoe's driveway, Gran says, "Now, if you don't want to call me, call Jace. Okay?"

Gran loves Jace and trusts him unconditionally. But I have no intention of calling him to pick me up for any reason.

On our way up to Wes's house, Zoe squeals, actually squeals, with delight when I show her what's in the bag Gran packed. I hear Foster the People playing from the back of the house. Good music is always a good sign. I ring the doorbell even though the front door is open. When no one answers, I figure everyone is in the back. We wander through the house, following the sound of the music and voices outside. I'd forgotten how huge the Jamisons' house is.

I take a look around when we step onto the porch. Apparently it's a fairly exclusive get-together, with only about a dozen people. Not at all like the party at Remy's. I immediately recognize Madeline, Emma, and Serena standing by the bar. Wes is behind it mixing drinks. He stops what he's doing when he sees me and jogs over to us.

"Pep! Hey! I'm glad you could make it." He gives me a hug and turns to shake Zoe's hand. "I'm Wesley."

"Hi! I'm Zoe." She is beaming.

I'm relieved that Wesley is okay with us being here. "Yeah, we, um, saw Pierce and Forbes earlier and they invited us. We brought stuff." I raise the brown paper grocery bag.

Wes raises his eyebrows when he looks inside. "Let me guess. Bunny?"

I laugh. "Yup. She said someone would know how to make margaritas."

"I think I can handle it. How is Bunny?" Wes asks. He takes the bag and guides us towards the bar. He places his hand on the small of my back and I notice Madeline glaring at me. Forbes and Pierce wave from the pool where they are playing pool basketball with two other guys. There are another half a dozen people on the beach chairs.

"Pep, Zoe, have you met Madeline, Serena, or Emma? They were at the party I saw you at the other night, Pepper." The girls look us over without saying anything. I gulp nervously.

"Yes, we met. We played beer pong. It's nice to see you guys again." I smile. I really hope they approve of us. We won't make it through this party if they don't like us.

Serena and Emma seem to defer to Madeline. They look at her and wait for her response. Madeline smiles tightly. "Yes, Pepper Jones, I remember. It's nice to see you too. Zoe, hi. What would you like to drink? Wes has a full bar."

Zoe pipes up. "Oh, we brought some stuff for margaritas. Do you want to whip those up, Wes, while I put out the chips and dip?" I widen my eyes. Wow. Zoe is smoother than I gave her credit for.

When I'm halfway through a margarita, I feel comfortable enough to take off my dress. Everyone else is in a bathing suit anyway. I sit on the edge of the pool and keep an eye on Zoe. She's lying on a recliner that floats in the water while Pierce stands beside her in the shallow end. Zoe has already finished one margarita and is on her second. I decide that this will be my only drink; I need to be the responsible one.

Wes sits down beside me. "How come you didn't race today?"

"I'm trying to make Nationals this year, which will make my season a lot longer than usual," I explain. "So I'm not going to start racing until later. You remember Ryan? You met him a couple of weeks ago."

Wes nods. "Yeah, he was with you at that party."

"He sat out the race too. He actually *won* Nationals last year."

"That's right, I heard about him. So, how do you qualify for Nationals?"

I splash some water in front of us with my feet and lean back on my hands. "At Regionals. There are four regions. The Midwest regionals are in Denver this year. Nationals are in San Diego. It'll be my first time on a plane if I make it."

Wes's phone beeps next to us and he takes a look at it. "I've got to go deal with something. I'll be back in a few minutes. You okay?" Wes puts his hand on mine gently before he gets up.

"Yeah, I'm fine. Just help me keep an eye on Zoe, will you? She doesn't drink much."

"No problem." Wes heads over to the shallow end of the pool and nods towards Pierce. Pierce hops out of the pool and talks to Wesley for a minute. They look at Zoe, who has her eyes closed on the raft. I notice her second margarita glass is empty.

After Wes tells Pierce not to take advantage of Zoe (at least, that's what I hope the conversation was about), he heads inside.

I can feel Madeline's eyes on me from the bar, where she sits on a stool surrounded by three guys. I try to avoid looking their way, but when I look in the other direction, I see Emma and Serena sitting on beach recliners watching me.

Pierce rejoins Zoe, though hopefully he won't refill her margarita or try to take her inside with him. Nobody is talking to me, and I'm no longer feeling comfortable sitting by myself on the poolside. I get up and wrap a towel around my waist before heading inside to the bathroom.

I hear Wes's voice in the study across from the bathroom, and I figure he must have taken a private phone call. Maybe it's his parents, who are out of town this weekend, and he doesn't want them to hear the party in the background.

I spend a moment looking in the mirror after I wash my hands. My long brown hair is pulled back in a ponytail. It's always wavier on a hot day like today, and a few wisps have escaped around my forehead. My big brown eyes stare back at me and I glance down at my body in my coral bikini. My skin tans nicely but I have a pretty brutal shorts tan line from all the running I did this summer. I look young and childish compared to the Lincoln Academy girls outside. I feel drab and boring, where they are girly and glamorous. I sigh. I should embrace the athletic running body I was given instead of wishing I had a different one. The grass is always greener. I'm mumbling this to myself when I open the bathroom door and nearly collide with a hard chest leaving the study.

I look up into green eyes. Jace's arms go around my waist to steady me. "Wesley, why is Pepper here?" Jace asks, his eyes locked on mine.

Wesley is leaving the study behind Jace. He scratches the back of his head. "Don't worry about it, man. My buddies saw her and her friend Zoe earlier today and invited them. There are only a few people over."

Jace's green eyes darken when he takes in my bikini. I haven't yet wrapped my towel back around my waist and I feel very exposed. Jace's hands stay on my waist, even though I no longer need them there to steady me. I wonder, is this what an older brother would do? Is that look in his eyes something more? Maybe Ryan was right.

Jace breaks eye contact and lets me go so abruptly that I stumble backward before bracing myself on the bathroom door. He looks over his shoulder at Wesley. "You got a bathing suit I can borrow?"

When Jace joins the party, Madeline immediately ditches the three boys at the bar and saunters over to him. I watch from my spot by the edge of the pool for a moment.

Jace blatantly admires her bikini-clad body, and his gaze rests for a moment on the little blue triangles that barely cover her boobs. She places a hand on his chest in greeting. I've seen enough. I take one more gulp of my margarita and dive into the pool.

I swim underwater all the way to the shallow end and pop up by Zoe's float. Pierce grins as I push my soaking wet hair out of my face. "You guys want to play water basketball?" I ask.

"Pepper!" Zoe whines. "I'm quite comfortable lying here nice and dry. You better not get me wet!"

"Aw, come on Zoe. You can be on my team, and we'll get Pepper a partner," Pierce says. I grab Zoe's drink and flick her with water. I take a sip and swim over to the edge to put it aside.

"Come on, Zoe! It'll be fun!" I call. She huffs, but slowly slides off her float.

"Hey Wes!" Pierce yells. Wes looks up from mixing a drink at the bar.

"Yo!" he calls back.

"Come play basketball. You're on Pepper's team."

Wes finishes making a drink and passes it to a girl standing nearby. Before he can join us, I hear Jace volunteer, "I'll play." He kicks off his flip-flops and walks straight to the edge of the pool to dive in. Madeline is left standing alone and she doesn't look pleased.

I feel hands grab my ankles and I can't help but squeal. His hands slide up my legs to my hips and before I know it I'm soaring through the air. I splash backwards in the deep end, my arms and legs flailing.

"Jace Vernon Wilder!" I scream as soon as I surface. He hates his middle name. I hear Wesley sputter and choke before erupting into laughter behind me.

I can see Jace's green eyes blaze from ten feet away. "You're in big trouble now," he threatens.

He starts towards me and I duck underwater, trying to swim away from him. I don't make it far before I feel strong hands wrap around my hips and launch me into the air again. There's not much I can do to retaliate, besides call him by his middle name. When we were younger, I used to pants him down to his underwear when he annoyed me, but I'm not sure how well that would work as a humiliation tactic these days. I'd probably end up more embarrassed than he would. Not to mention, we're in a pool, and he's not wearing underwear.

Jace grins at me and, as usual, I melt a little. "Truce?" he asks.

I cross my arms defiantly. "It's not like I have a choice. I can't exactly toss you in the air."

He swims back over to me. "Yeah, but you can call me by my middle name and you know how much that pisses me off," he tells me as he adjusts my bathing suit strap. "As soon as I turn eighteen I'm changing it."

"What are you going to change it to?"

"I haven't decided yet. Got any ideas?" My eyes can't help but rest on his chest, where his muscles flex each time he moves in the water. The sun glistens off his wet skin and I follow a drop of water from his shoulder down past his nipple and over the defined ridges of his six-pack.

"I'm all wet now!" Zoe interrupts after dunking her head under water. "Let's play!"

The game goes on for a while, and everyone else at the party wants to get in on it once they see how much fun we're having. We rotate teams, letting the winner stay on. Of course, with Jace as my teammate, we never lose.

"Damn, Pepper. I knew you were a good runner, but maybe you should pick up basketball too," Forbes tells me after we beat him and Serena for the second time.

"It's all Jace," I insist.

"No it's not." Jace throws his arm around me. "I'm pretty sure you've been sinking just as many hoops. Let's call it though, I'm hungry." Before I know it, Jace has dropped under the water and lifted me onto his shoulders.

With his head between my legs, I can't help but feel like maybe, just maybe, this was a flirtatious move. But I flash back to the big brother talk we had just weeks ago, and the conversation I heard in the locker room, and give myself a mental head slap. I want to run my hands through his hair, but I place them on his strong shoulders instead.

I see Wesley making his way over to the porch, where two tough-looking guys are walking towards the pool area. Wesley glances nervously at Jace, who lowers himself down in the water and gently moves my legs off his shoulders. He turns to look at me and puts his hands on my own shoulders.

"Bunny expecting you for dinner?" he asks.

"No, I told her I didn't know when we'd be home. She told me to call whenever we're ready."

"We're grilling burgers here. If you want to stay, I can give you and Zoe a ride home later." His hands are rubbing up and down my arms and it feels so nice. I just want to take one step closer and lean into his chest. But I don't.

"Yeah. That'd be great." I try to sound casual but my heart is beating rapidly. Jace is not only touching me and standing shirtless in front of me, but he actually invited me to stay and hang out with his friends. I smile at him.

"You're getting goosebumps. Do you have dry clothes to change into?"

I shake my head. "I just brought a dress to go over my suit, but I can't wear it without any underwear. And I didn't bring any."

Jace just stares at me.

"Underwear, that is," I clarify. "I have a big beach towel I'll use until I dry off. Poor planning on my part," I add with a shrug.

"It's gonna get cold when the sun goes down. I'll get a sweatshirt from my car."

"You don't have to," I tell him, knowing he will anyway. He ignores me and takes my hand.

"Where's your towel?" I point to a patio chair and he guides me to it. He takes out the towel and quickly wraps it around me. I notice the tough guys on the patio are watching him. I recognize one of them from the day I saw Jace tubing on the river.

"Who are those guys?" I ask Jace.

"Just some UC guys I hang out with sometimes. But they aren't good news, Pep, so don't go making new friends."

"If they're bad news, why do you hang out with them?" I turn and look at him. His green eyes are even sexier when his eyelashes are wet.

Jace sighs. "It's complicated."

I raise my eyebrows, awaiting further explanation.

He shakes his head a little. "Don't push it, Pep. I'm going to my car to get you some clothes." He tosses me my cell phone from my bag. "Give Buns a call and tell her I'll get you home tonight."

I make a quick call to Gran, who tells me I sound far too sober. "Jace'll keep an eye on you. Tell him I told him to make you another margarita. They're good, don't you think?"

"Zoe certainly thinks so." I watch her stumble a little as she climbs out of the pool, with Pierce still tagging along beside her.

After my phone call, I lie back on the patio chair and pull the beach towel tighter around me. The sun is fading, and the sky is turning a light shade of pink. I look up into the clouds, and a shadow hovers over me. I blink. It's one of the UC guys. He has a black tee shirt on that stretches tightly across defined muscles. His dark hair is buzzed short, and the smile on his face does nothing to soften his hard features.

He sits on the chair next to mine. "I'm Wolfe." I smirk. What an appropriate name.

I remember Jace's warning, but there's not much I can do short of ignore the guy. "I'm Pepper." I sit up, deciding I should make my way over to the bar and grill, where Wesley is with the other UC guy, and there are others around.

He holds my elbow as I stand up and I can't help but flinch. "So, you and Jace, huh?"

"What do you mean?" I ask warily.

He shrugs. "I've seen Jace with a lot of girls. Never had him stare me down like he just did when I checked *you* out." Wolfe winks. I narrow my eyes.

"Yeah, well, we've been friends a long time. He keeps an eye out for me." Hopefully he catches the implication that I'm not interested.

"In that case, no one has a claim on you, huh? I can check you out all I want?" I wrap my towel more tightly around me, and see Jace coming out from the house with a bundle of clothes.

"I'm changing, so you lost your opportunity."

I walk towards Jace, who clenches his jaw and glares at Wolfe over my shoulder. His eyes dart to me and soften slightly. But he still looks angry. "I guess you didn't listen?"

"I did. I tried not to encourage friendship." I try to look back without being obvious. "Is he sticking around? He kind of creeps me out."

Jace hands me a pile of clothes. "I think that's the plan. Rex is manning the grill over there and they came together. I should ask them to leave." Jace looks at me, awaiting my opinion.

"It's not worth it. I'm going to change," I decide.

I put on a pair of baggy basketball shorts that fall to my calves and tie the string as tight I can around my waist. I pull Jace's hoodie over my head and don't bother looking in the mirror. I'm sure I look ridiculous. Although I certainly don't look sexy, strangely enough, I feel all kinds of sexy with my naked skin underneath Jace's clothes, knowing his skin has been on it too. I roll my eyes at my wayward thoughts as I walk down the hallway and join the others on the patio.

Jace is sitting on a patio chair drinking a beer. He smiles and asks me to sit with him.

"On your lap, Jace?" I ask doubtfully.

"Yes. You look adorable right now." He pulls me towards him. I am so utterly confused. I know exactly what I want this gesture to mean, but I have no idea if he is on the same page. Adorable, huh?

"Don't get too comfortable. Gran ordered you to make me a margarita. Apparently I'm too sober, and you will watch out for me if I get drunk." I turn and look at him. "She trusts you."

"She should," Jace says. "With you, at least."

"I trust you too." We are inches apart and I lean forward just enough to touch my forehead to his. I want to communicate so much more than that. I stare at him, hoping he'll recognize what I feel but can't say. He squeezes his arms around my back. For a moment, I see something in those green eyes that looks familiar, because I'm sure it's what's reflected in my own eyes.

"You guys want cheese on your burgers?" the guy at the grill asks, interrupting the moment. I had completely forgotten the world around us for those few seconds.

"Yeah, thanks Rex," Jace says.

"Same."

"Hey Wes, can you make Pep a margarita?" Jace calls to Wes at the bar.

"You liked that last one I made, huh?" He grins.

I nudge Jace. "You lazy-ass."

"Nah, I'm just comfortable." He squeezes me again. "How many have you had?"

"Just the one when we got here hours ago." I tap his beer bottle. "Don't drink too many. You're the driver."

"Thanks, Pepper. You know I can take care of myself though, right?" he says playfully.

"Yeah, yeah."

"If you start coming around with me, is this what it's gonna be like? You scoldin' me?"

"I wasn't scolding!" I grin, delighted that he is considering that this might become a regular occurrence. "Besides, you're the one who gets all big brother bear on me."

Jace swallows a sip of beer and frowns. The silence that passes is awkward. After all, I'm sitting on his lap, and I just brought up his brotherly feelings towards me.

I don't know what to think or feel anymore. I thought I'd finally figured it out, but now I'm questioning everything. I get up and walk to the bar to get my drink from Wes. I sit on a stool with my back to Jace. I need a moment.

"Thanks, Wes." I take a huge gulp of the drink.

"Easy there, Killer." Wes pats my hand.

I hang at the bar with Wes, and keep an eye on Zoe. Pierce seems genuinely interested in her, and isn't being a creeper. Wolfe doesn't approach me again. When Wes heads into the house for something, Madeline takes the stool next to mine.

"Hi." She looks directly at me.

"Hi." I swallow. With her perfect hair flowing around her shoulders and her confident demeanor, I can't help but feel intimidated.

"I saw you talking to Wolfe. You know those guys?"

"Uh, no. I just met him."

"Yeah, I didn't think so. They don't hang with a good crowd." She glances over her shoulder. "I didn't think Jace would be down with you hanging with them. I guess he's okay with you hanging with us though, huh?"

I frown. "How do you know anything about Jace?"

Her eyes widen in surprise before she lets out a startled laugh.

"I mean, I, uh," I stutter, realizing how bitchy I must have sounded. You don't do bitchy around Madeline Brescoll unless you want to get caught in her net. "It's just, you know, I just met you. We don't really know each other. Maybe I do hang out with a bad crowd, right?"

She continues chuckling and shaking her head. "You're a funny girl, Pepper."

I stare at her, awaiting further explanation.

"And a little clueless," she adds. Before she can elaborate, Jace is behind my stool.

"Ready, Pep?" He squeezes my shoulders. "I'll get your stuff. Wanna grab Zoe?"

"Sure." I glance once more at Madeline, who still has an amused look on her face. She checks out Jace's bum, and my own eyes follow her gaze, as he walks away. I sigh.

"Too hot for his own good, don't you think?" Madeline says softly.

I clear my throat. I'm not supposed to feel this way about Jace. "I guess. Nice to see you, Madeline. See you around."

She just smiles at me and nods. I grab Zoe, who exchanges numbers eagerly with Pierce before we leave.

After dropping off Zoe, we head to Jace's house. Jim is watching ESPN in the living room with a Budweiser in his hand. "Pepper!" he exclaims. "It's good to see you." He envelops me in a bear hug.

"Hi Jim." Jim's the closest I have to a father. I don't see him too often, but I know he's always around if I need him.

Jace takes my hand and pulls me towards the stairs. "We'll be downstairs, Dad." I follow him to the basement, where he has his own bedroom, bathroom, and entertainment area. It's a modest ranch house, but with just the two of them, Jace has a lot of space to himself.

"Want something to drink?" He opens his mini fridge and pulls out a beer. "Apple juice?"

"Yup." Jace knows I love apple juice. Especially when it's in those little juice boxes with a straw. He unwraps the straw and pops it into the box before handing it to me.

Jace plops himself on the black beanbag in the corner of his bedroom and takes a long sip of beer. He watches me, and I can't bring myself to look away. I stand in the middle of his room, lips touching the straw of the juice box. The air in the room is thick, and my breaths are shallow. A low hum vibrates through my body. It starts in my core and pulses to the tips of my fingers and down my legs. Does Jace feel it too?

"We never started the Hendrix puzzle," he says.

I blink. Oh. Right. Of course he doesn't feel it.

"I'm not really in the mood for a puzzle," I tell him. I can't make eye contact. I place the juice box on Jace's dresser and pull my hair off my neck. My skin is hot; I need relief, so I pile my hair on my head.

"Do you have a rubber band?" I ask him, scanning the top of his dresser.

"Don't think so. You can check my desk drawer."

I sit at his desk chair and pull open drawers, anything to distract me from the buzzing in my body, my head, the air that I'm breathing. How can he not feel it too?

"No rubber bands," I say with a sigh, dropping my hands from my hair and letting it fall down my back. I lean back against the chair and stare in front of me.

"A movie, then?" he asks.

My eyes dart in his direction before I can help it. Maybe it was something in the tone of his voice that made me look at him. But I catch it. The look that Ryan was talking about. I don't know how to describe it, or exactly what I'm seeing. All I know is that it might be the first time I've ever seen Jace Wilder look defenseless. I've always sensed some vulnerability buried deep within him, and I know it has to do with his mother jumping ship when he was four years old. So what brought it on now?

The softness in his green eyes glazes over again, and the cool, controlled Jace is back in place. Did I imagine it? Maybe it's the tequila making me bold, but I suddenly can't stop myself. I stand up slowly.

"Not in the mood for a movie either," I say quietly.

It's time to find out once and for all if Jace really thinks of me like a sister, or if Ryan's conviction that it's something more holds any truth. I'll either crush all hopes for good, or... what? My brain can't process any further than its want, its need, to be closer to Jace. I walk towards him.

His lips part ever so slightly. His face is still a mask of calm, but he's holding his breath, and that gives him away.

I stand in front of him for just an instant before placing a knee on either side of his hips. I'm straddling him, but we aren't touching.

Jace puts his beer down and places his hands on my hips. "Pepper? What are you doing?"

It's that vulnerability again. This time in his voice. If I didn't know him so well, I wouldn't hear it.

I let my hands tangle in the hair that I've wanted to touch so many times. Jace's eyes drift closed. I lean my head in and brush my lips back and forth against his.

He's stopped holding his breath, and is now breathing heavily. I lower myself onto his lap, and that's when I know for sure. I can feel him through his swim trunks. He definitely does not think of me like a sister.

I push my tongue in his mouth, urging him to open to me. He complies, and lets me explore, but he doesn't respond. His grip on my hips is feather-light. If it wasn't for the growing hardness pressed against my thigh, I would think he was unaffected.

I continue to clutch his hair in my hands, and when my hips shift slightly, Jace's hands squeeze me tighter. His tongue begins to massage mine, and he shifts in the beanbag so that I can feel him right at my core. Whoa.

I've never been this close to a boy before, but my body knows exactly what to do. My hips move forward and back, creating a delightful friction. There's just skin underneath Jace's gym shorts, and the silky material slides with me as I rock back and forth.

Jace's hands begin to wander. Over my bottom, up my stomach, and to my breasts, which are uncovered beneath his sweatshirt. His thumbs rub gently over the curves in rhythm with our massaging tongues and rocking hips.

Jace breaks our kiss, but doesn't say anything as he moves his lips to my neck. His hands continue to wander, and I can feel his hot breath move along my collarbone. It's all so instinctive. My body has a life of its own, and I'm feeling desperate for something, I don't know what.

I press harder into him, seeking the delicious friction rubbing at my center. Pressure is building slowly in my belly. It keeps tightening and I groan in both frustration and ecstasy.

Jace seems to understand, and he grabs my hips again, guiding me against him. Our foreheads mush together as we rock frantically in a natural rhythm that feels so right. Suddenly the tension and pressure building inside me explodes.

Strange, wanton cries leave my lips. My entire body quivers and shakes and I realize Jace is kissing me to smother the noise I'm making. I continue to rock against him as I tumble, a feeling of total and complete ecstasy exploding from my core and tingling throughout my body.

Jace's breathing is ragged and a deep frown creases his eyebrows as though he's concentrating hard. I watch, fascinated, as his eyes widen and he gasps before closing them tightly. He squeezes my bottom and thrusts up hard against me several times before shuddering.

I drop my head to the crook of his neck. Our chests rise and fall together for several minutes. My mind is spinning, and I don't want to come back to reality.

"I can't believe you just made me come in my pants, Pepper." He sounds utterly astonished, and slightly ashamed.

I smile against his neck. "I came in mine. Well, yours."

He brushes damp hair from my forehead and kisses me lightly on the top of my head. "Have you ever done that before?" he asks gently.

"I don't know which part you're asking about. It wasn't my first kiss. But everything else was a first." I keep my head buried in his neck, embarrassed in spite of what we just shared. This is Jace Wilder, after all. He's been doing this for years with who knows how many girls.

"It was a first for me, too," he says heavily.

I raise my head and look at him with a frown. "Huh?"

"I've never lost control like that, I mean. I've never, you know, blown my load from making out," Jace says on a hard swallow.

Is Jace Wilder embarrassed? I open my mouth to tease him but quickly shut it. He looks so serious, and confused. And now, that lost boy look I caught a glimpse of is plainly etched on his face. He's letting me see it.

Not for long, though. Jace shuts his eyes and leans his head back, banging it on the wall behind him. "Fuck."

I have no idea what I expected, but it's clear he's not happy about what just happened. I start to crawl off of him. Jace doesn't move, and his eyes remain closed. I walk over to the dresser and take a sip of apple juice. My body zings with energy but my brain is in a stupor.

"That can't happen again," Jace says from the bean bag. His serious, controlled voice is back. Unwanted emotions locked away and buried deep once again.

I look over my shoulder at him. He's now leaning forward, shoulders hunched, elbows on knees. "Why not?" I know before I ask that I won't get an explanation. He's closed off now, and he's got his determined look on.

"It just can't," he says shortly. He stands up abruptly, ending the conversation. Without looking at me, he walks towards his bedroom door. "Come on, I'll walk you home."

I might still be in a stupor, but I know what a Jace Wilder rejection looks like. I've seen him do it to plenty of people. But never me. Another first.

"Don't bother." I brush past him and run quickly up the stairs. "Later, Jim!" I call as I fly out the front door.

The door doesn't shut when I slam it behind me, and I know Jace is standing there, having followed me up the stairs. I walk home quickly, feeling his gaze on me the whole way.

Chapter 10

Gran gives me a confused look when we hear a knock at the door on Monday morning. Jace never knocks. I harden my heart and open the door, only to find Remy standing there. "What's up, Pepper?"

"Uh, where's Jace?"

"Oh, he didn't call you?" He scratches his head. "He had to go out of town for something, so he asked me to pick you up for school."

Gran harrumphs from the breakfast table. I wave to her and follow Remy to his car. Connor is sitting in the back seat.

"Hey, Pepper," he greets me. "How was your weekend?"

I glance at him. "It was okay I guess." It was amazing and heartbreaking all at once is what it was.

When Remy settles in the front seat I turn towards the center so I'm partly facing both of them. "So, I hear you guys talked to Ryan about me?"

Remy peeks at Connor in the rear view mirror and tightens the steering wheel. "Jace doesn't know we did that, Pep. Don't be mad at him."

"I'm not. I didn't say anything to him about it. But seriously, why did you do that?"

Connor speaks up. "Come on, Pepper. You have to know how Jace is about you. Ryan didn't get it. You can't blame him. He's new and all."

"What? Because Jace is my friend and has a temper, no guy can go out with me?"

Remy coughs. "Yeah. Sort of."

Connor adds, "It's a little more than that, but yeah, that's the gist. We thought Ryan should get the picture."

"That's the stupidest thing I've ever heard." It's not. Not exactly. Jace can be pretty scary and his friends wouldn't want anything going on that encourages his volatile behavior. The guy likes control. And for the most part, he controls whatever he wants in his world. Apparently I'm not an exception.

"Don't act like this is news, Pepper. You have to know you're hot. Really hot." Remy shoots him a warning glare from the rear view mirror. "But, do guys ever go for you?"

"Charlie asked me to prom last year," I tell him.

Remy laughs. "Yeah, well, I think Jace knows you and Charlie are just friends."

I cross my arms over my chest. I'm furious. Not so much at Jace's controlling attitude, which isn't exactly news, but that I seem to have been the only one oblivious to its impact on my own life. I guess I haven't been entirely oblivious. Willful ignorance may be more accurate. It hasn't really mattered until now. Actually, it's been kind of nice not having boys distracting me.

But now, I want Ryan distracting me. If I can't have Jace, I want Ryan. I know I'm acting like a two year old, but it sure doesn't seem fair that Jace can reject me and keep me from seeing anyone else at the same time.

Connor puts a hand on my shoulder. "We just thought Ryan should know what he was getting into. A stirred up Jace Wilder isn't a good thing."

"Guys!" I throw my hands up. "I talked to Jace about Ryan! He was cool with it. Jace can see Ryan's a good guy." It was a done deal now, but I wanted to prevent this from happening again. "Just, stay out of it next time, okay? I'm sorry if what I do makes Jace less cool to be around for you guys, but I can handle him."

Remy nods. "Okay. But it's not just about being less cool. We can handle him too."

Connor snorts. "Not always."

"It doesn't matter anymore anyway," I tell them. "At least not with Ryan. We're just friends. But next time, if there is one, just let me handle it, okay?"

"Yeah, okay," Connor grumbles.

"Sure, Pepper," Remy says as he turns up the music.

These guys have been Jace's wingmen since his freshman year, and they take their loyalty to him pretty seriously. I know they won't listen to me unless Jace tells them to.

When Wesley went to Lincoln, and he and Jace stopped hanging out, it didn't take long for others to pledge their allegiance. Jace is one of those guys who attracts people, guys and girls alike, without even trying. I am not immune. But oh, how I wish I was.

★ ★ ★

Zoe runs up to me at lunch before I can sit at our table. "Ah! I missed you at your locker this morning! You will not believe what I have to tell you."

Claire, Charlie, Rollie and Omar look up as we approach. Zoe's dramatics are nothing new, but this time it sounds personal.

Charlie raises his eyebrows. "We already heard about Wes's party. How was it?"

Zoe slams her brown bag lunch on the table and plops in her seat. "Awesome. Totally awesome. Pierce Malone was there. Do you know him?" Everyone nods dutifully. "I hung out with him and we had a really good time. He was super nice and cool. So, he got my number and he called last night to see if we could do something together this week."

"That's awesome, Zoe. He did seem really into you," I add.

Zoe dumps the contents out from her lunch sack and starts sorting through it. "Yeah, well, we made plans for Thursday after practice. But when I told my dad, he totally flipped out." Zoe's dad's a cop and kind of a hardass.

"Why? He's let you see guys before, hasn't he?" Charlie asks.

"He asked how I knew Pierce and I had to admit that I wasn't just over at your house on Saturday, Pepper, but that we hung out with him at Wesley Jamison's house for a little while. I didn't tell him there was underage drinking, just that he had a pool and we went swimming."

"So what's the problem?" I ask.

"He just said that Wesley and Pierce are bad news and he doesn't want me hanging around them anymore." She looks pointedly in my direction. "He doesn't think you should hang around them either and he threatened to call Bunny to say something. But don't worry, I talked him out of it."

Omar asks the question that we're all thinking. "Why are they bad news? They're rich kids who play football. They don't get into trouble."

Zoe lowers her voice. "I'm probably not supposed to say anything. Actually, I know I'm not supposed to." She glances around conspiratorially. "My dad got real evasive and wouldn't explain anything, just stomped off. But I heard him talking to my mom later about how Wesley almost got busted for dealing drugs last year."

"Whoa," Rollie says.

"What kind of drugs?" Omar asks. "I mean, if it was just pot, that's not that big of a deal. It's practically legal anyway," he adds.

Charlie asks, "Were they smoking at the party?"

"I didn't see anyone smoking or anyone on drugs," I tell them. "Did you?" I ask Zoe.

She shakes her head. "No. That's why it's so weird."

"Why would he deal drugs? Isn't he loaded?" Rollie asks.

"Yeah, he is. I don't get it," Charlie answers.

We are all quiet for a moment, processing the information.

"Maybe it's just a rumor, and your dad's being overprotective," Omar suggests.

"So no date then, huh?" I ask. She seems more intrigued by the drug rumor than she is disappointed about not going on a date with Pierce.

Zoe shrugs and takes a bite of sandwich. "No. My dad would freak. It's not worth it."

"Aren't you bummed about Pierce though?" Claire asks, her cheeks reddening. "He's really cute."

Zoe giggles. "This is true. But, whatever."

This is why I love this girl. She never takes anything too seriously. I, on the other hand, can't help but notice Jace's empty seat at the popular table. He's out of town and didn't even tell me where he was going. I wonder just how much of his life I'm kept out of. Perhaps it's better this way.

★ ★ ★

On the way home from practice, Ryan asks about my weekend and I tell him about the pool party at Wes's house. "It was cool, I guess. How about you? What'd you do after our meet on Saturday?" I ask him.

Ryan looks out the window. "Oh, just a party at some girl's house I didn't know. There are tons of parties at this school. More than my old school. But Brockton's three times the size. I guess with that many people, there's always someone's parents out of town."

"Was it fun?" Stupidly, I'm a little disappointed he didn't at least text me to let me know. I thought we were becoming pretty good friends, despite our failed attempt to make it something more at the beginning.

"Yeah, it was okay." He shifts in his seat before glancing at me. "I was going to call you, but, you know. . ." He drifts off.

"You can still call me and we can still do things together, even if it's not going to be something more between us," I tell him.

"Yeah, okay. Sorry. But you wouldn't have been able to go anyway, right?"

"True," I concede. "So, Lisa Delaney's really into you." Maybe I shouldn't go there, but I can't help my curiosity. Has he totally given up on me and moved on?

Ryan sighs. "I know. I'm not really into her though."

I smile to myself. If Jace isn't going to let anything happen with us, why shouldn't I go for a great guy like Ryan?

He pulls up outside my apartment. "Anyway, I know Jace wasn't around at school today. Maybe I can come in and say hi to Bunny, if there's an extra seat at the table?" Ryan asks.

My smile broadens. I'm happy for the distraction from Jace's unexplained absence. "Gran would love that."

Bunny is bustling about the kitchen when we open the door. "Ryan! It's nice to see you again. I thought I'd scared you off." She hugs him.

"No, I had a great time before. I hope you don't mind me joining you tonight."

"As long as you like shepherd's pie. And I made brownies for dessert. Don't tell me you can't eat it. You runners need the extra fat. You'll be getting a healthy spoonful of ice cream too."

Ryan laughs. "That'd be great. Thank you, Bunny."

We're passing the shepherd's pie around when Jace walks in. He looks tired. I see his reaction through the opening between the counter and the cabinets when he notices Ryan in his seat. Jace doesn't look angry, but resigned.

Ryan pushes back from his seat when Jace comes around to the table. "Oh, hey Jace." He offers him his chair.

"It's cool, man." Jace puts his hand on Ryan's shoulder. "I'll pull up a chair. Is there enough for me, Buns?"

"Of course, dear. Let me get another place setting." Bunny starts to stand up but Jace nudges her back to her seat.

"Sit down. I got it. Sorry to interrupt." Jace goes into the kitchen and opens the cabinet for a glass.

We are quiet at the table. I glance at Ryan, who is shifting around in his seat. When Jace sits at the table and starts dishing food onto his plate like it's a totally normal night, we all relax a little.

"So, Jace," Gran says. "How come a boy I never met was here to get Pepper this morning instead of you?"

"Sorry, Buns. He's a good friend. Pepper knows him." He takes a sip of milk and pats Dave, who rests his head on Jace's thigh.

Gran tsks. "That didn't answer my question, young man."

"I had to go out of town to take care of something," Jace says. He holds Gran's gaze, and they have a staring match for a moment. Jace still hasn't answered her question and he knows it.

Gran accepts his vague response, but not before asking one more question. "And why didn't you let Pepper know you were out of town? We all have phones nowadays."

Jace looks at me. "Sorry, Pep," he says softly. "It was sort of last minute."

Gran shakes her head, because he didn't answer that question either. But I already know the answer. He's keeping his distance. Instituting boundaries. Controlling our relationship. What's new?

Jace changes the subject. "So, I'm actually gonna be out of town a bunch this fall for a couple of recruit visits to different colleges. I'll usually just be gone weekends, but I'll have Remy swing by if I'm away on a school day."

The dinner with both Ryan and Jace isn't quite as bad as I'd thought it'd be. The guys end up talking about the different colleges they are visiting on recruiting trips, and Gran chirps in with her opinions.

"Are either of you guys considering CU?" I ask. I haven't raised the subject with Jace, but I've wanted to a million times. I take a bite of mashed potatoes, pretending to be more interested in the food than his answer.

"Yeah, definitely," Ryan answers first. "It was one of my first choices before my dad became coach. It's got one of the best cross programs in the country. So, assuming my dad doesn't screw that up, I'll just have to decide if I want him to be my coach."

"Would that be weird?" I ask.

"I don't think so. He's always helped coach me unofficially. I think it could be pretty cool," he says with a shrug. "We'll see. I haven't gone on any other visits yet so maybe I'll like somewhere else better. Oregon seems pretty awesome too."

Gran helps me out. "What about you, Jace?" She asks him.

Jace looks right at me. "CU's my first choice."

I put my fork down. "But you just told us about all the schools recruiting you. I don't get it. I didn't think CU's football team was in the same league."

"It's not. But it still has a decent division one team. I'd rather know I'm gonna get to play than risk being a bench warmer." Jace watches me as he butters a piece of cornbread.

"Hmmm. . ." Gran hums loudly from her end of the table.

"What about you, Pep?" Jace asks. "What are you thinking for college?"

I'm surprised by his question. I figured he knew I wouldn't want to leave Gran.

"CU, if they gave me a scholarship. If not, the closest school with a running team that gives me a scholarship." I pat Gran's hand. "Don't worry, I'll move into the dorms at least."

"You know you can stay here with me on Shadow Lane as long as you want, baby girl," Gran tells me.

Jace only stays a moment to help clean up after Ryan leaves. I'm still digesting the news that he might stay in Brockton. I almost wish I didn't know it was a possibility. I don't want to get my hopes up. Besides, he'll be in college. I'll never see him. Kids from Brockton go to CU all the time, but they disappear just like the kids who go out of state. Swept into the college bubble. It's another reason why it's so odd that Jace hangs out with college kids. That world is supposed to be separate.

Gran can tell I'm distracted and she doesn't ask me about homework or anything else. Instead, she takes her nightly bong hit and settles in to watch television and knit on the sofa with Dave.

Chapter 11

The rest of the week falls into its normal routine. Jace picks me up in the morning, mostly ignores me at school, and eats dinner at our house a few nights. I'm starting to wonder if I imagined everything that happened on Saturday night.

If I'm being honest, I guess things aren't totally the same between us. I want to pretend that we can go back to our easy friendship, but I can't. Making out with Jace was one of the best moments of my life, followed by one of the worst. It was hard enough trying to ignore my feelings for him before I kissed him. Now that I know firsthand how good it can be with us, suppressing my wayward thoughts when we're together is impossible. Besides, Jace felt it too. That was undeniable.

So why did he say it can't happen again?

I have some theories. He doesn't stick around with one girl, and he cares about me enough not to want to hurt me, which he undoubtedly will. Maybe he doesn't want our friendship to change, since we've got a pretty good thing going with the whole keeping it platonic thing. Plus, he doesn't do the girlfriend thing, and he knows I'm not a casual hook up kind of girl. I can understand those explanations. But I expect there's something more. If it felt as good for him as it did for me, he'd be willing to take the risk. Right?

Jace wants to control our relationship just like he does everything else in his life. He's controlled it so far, I'll be the first to admit. Keeping our friendship in a neat little box, separate from the rest of his crazy party life. And I'm not the only one he keeps at arms' length. He never gets emotionally involved with a girl, despite his intimate interactions with them. How does he do that anyway? On the beanbag in his room, I felt closer to him than I ever had before. Minutes later, when he coldly told me it wouldn't happen again, I felt lonelier than I ever had before. Talk about an emotional rollercoaster.

The arrival of my first race of the season – the Aspen Leaf Invitational – forces me to stop overanalyzing Jace Wilder and the havoc he's wreaking on my heart.

Unfortunately, Dorothy Sandoval is my teammate, and she has juicy gossip to share.

"Did you hear about what happened at Ben's place on Thursday night?" It's a rhetorical question. Dorothy knows that no one on the team is friends with that crowd, or keeps tabs on them.

"I guess it was a just a few people," she continues when no one responds. "You know the group. Connor, Remy, Jace, Kayla, Andrea, and Lisa. Oh, and Tina Anderson. You know she's kind of dating Connor or something now right? Well, they all did E."

"E? Are we supposed to know what that is?" Jenny asks.

"It's ecstasy. You know, like the drug. They're little pills you take and they make you really, like, happy and sensual and stuff," Dorothy is all too eager to inform us.

"Oh," Jenny says in a tone suggesting she doesn't especially care to be educated by Dorothy Sandoval on the matter.

I swallow, the cool morning air no longer feeling as refreshing as it did just a moment ago. Jace told me he didn't do drugs. I thought I could at least believe the things he does tell me, even if I have to be left to wonder about the things he doesn't.

"Yeah. *Ohhhhh*," Dorothy emphasizes dramatically, before continuing her story. "And I guess they were all like, tripping out, and one thing led to another, and there was a lot of sex."

My throat tightens and constricts and it has nothing to do with our jogging pace, which should feel easy and relaxing. I stumble over a root.

"You okay?" Zoe asks.

I regain my footing. "Yeah. How do you know about this?" I ask Dorothy.

"Tina Anderson. You know, Dana Foster's BFF? They're in my photography class and we sometimes hang out. I mean, they're juniors, but they're cool," Dorothy adds. I glance at Zoe, who rolls her eyes. Dorothy's point that *we* are not cool enough does not go unnoticed.

She continues proudly relaying her information. "Tina and Dana said that this wasn't the first time the group had that kind of get-together, but Tina was only invited for the first time the other night. She said she'd try to see if Dana could come next time. But seriously, if she's telling people all about it, I doubt they'll invite her again."

I clear the lump in my throat. "So, what did she mean about a lot of sex?"

Claire, who is running beside me, gives me an annoyed look. We usually ignore Dorothy's little rants, and it's unlike me to encourage her. But I can't help my curiosity.

"It sounded like they all had sex with each other. How crazy is that, right? Okay, maybe not everyone had sex with everyone, but, like, they watched and stuff. Tina saw Jace bang all three of the other girls. She made it sound like he didn't go for her because she was with Connor, but I think she was kind of disappointed."

Zoe snorts. "Seriously? That's pathetic. Who wants to get in line for that? Yuck!"

I'm disgusted, and hurt. But this shouldn't affect me so much because I've always known how Jace is, right? No, this isn't the Jace I've always known. Sex with multiple girls in one night? Hard drugs like ecstasy? A simple kiss and make out session with me is nothing to him. I'm not cut out to be with a guy like Jace. I'm only fit to be his neighborly friend, separate from the world he lives in.

And the thing is, I want no part of that world. It's not the Jace I know, the Jace I've had a crush on for years. Who is he anyway? Do I even know him?

My head is swimming and the trees in front of me start to blur. I quickly wipe my eyes before anyone can see, but they immediately refill with hot tears.

Claire notices before I can turn away and she touches my arm. I slow my pace to drop to the back of the group. The last thing I want is Dorothy catching my reaction and adding it to the gossip circuit.

"Hey, hey," Claire says softly, noticing the tears burning down my cheeks. "What's going on?" She searches my eyes.

"It's nothing." I wipe my running nose and take deep breaths to calm myself.

Zoe looks behind her and catches my eye. I nod, urging her to keep the team from noticing me. Bless her little wild heart, Zoe asks Dorothy a question, distracting her from my melt down.

I stop running, and Claire rubs my back, unsure why she's comforting me, but doing it nonetheless.

I kick some rocks and look up at the sky. "I can't help it. I know he's not in my league, but. . ." I sigh. "I kissed Jace last weekend, and I thought he was into it. The kiss, it changed everything for me. But obviously, it didn't for him."

Zoe pulls me in for a hug. I blubber on her shoulder. "I feel like I don't even know him sometimes."

"Maybe Dorothy misheard or misunderstood what Tina was saying," Claire says quietly.

"Why would Tina make something like that up?" I pull away. "And you know Dorothy has no reason to embellish a story for our benefit. Besides, I've heard rumors about the same kind of thing before, it just never bothered me like it does now. Before he was just my friend who was unattainable, and the rumors were just stories about the side of him I'd never know," I say with a frustrated sigh. "I thought, maybe, after we kissed, that I could know all of him, you know? But now I don't know if I want to know all of him, or if I even can."

"I always knew you and Jace had this weird friendship but you never talk about it, so I never knew how it was."

"Well, I don't really know how it is either." I laugh bitterly. "I shouldn't have kissed him. It just gave me an even more real visual when I hear about him with other girls."

When Claire doesn't say anything in response, I know she agrees. I'm not one of those girls, and a hot guy like Jace Wilder has no reason to treat me differently from the many other girls he can be with. I should have just kept it platonic.

The joy of racing eases the throbbing in my chest to a dull ache. Fortunately, the physical reaction of heartbreak doesn't mess with the strength in my legs. Just like Coach instructed, I settle in to a comfortable tempo, letting my legs carry me along.

"Bring it in, Pepper!" I hear Coach call from the sideline. "Nice and steady."

I detect the warning in his voice, urging me not to push too hard. There's no reason to. I'm leading the race, and there's no sound of anyone behind me.

"Yaaaaaay Pepper!" Gran screams when I run by her on the final stretch to the finish line. She's jumping up and down and I grin in her direction.

I'm still grinning when I run through the finish line. It's the first race I've won with such ease. My time is several seconds faster than my time on this course last year, and I'm not even breathing very hard. It's just what I need - confidence that Nationals is within my reach. The season technically began a month ago, but I was just in waiting mode until now.

I cheer my teammates on when they finish, and we warm down together before watching the boys' race. There are two guys from other teams who stay with Ryan for the first two miles but he drops them easily and they fall back with the rest of the pack. Ryan doesn't even look like he's at a race. His long legs move smoothly, as though running is the most natural thing in the world. God made this boy's body to run, and it's beautiful to watch.

"He's like you, you know." Jenny is standing next to me at the finish line. "He's like the boy version of you when he runs. Have you ever watched yourself run?" she asks.

I frown. "Actually no, I don't think so. I've seen pictures."

"Yeah, well, you look totally awesome when you're running. I watched you at state last year when I was still in eighth grade." She grins. "I was kind of obsessed."

I like this girl. There's no facade. No fear. She runs that way too. "You kicked butt today, by the way. What place was it? Fifth? That's awesome."

"Thanks." She beams. Jenny beat Zoe and Claire. She's already moved into the number two position on the team as a freshman. I'm excited to watch her improve even more.

Ryan finds me after the race and introduces me to his mom and his thirteen-year-old brother, Kevin. Before I have a chance to talk to them, we are interrupted by a guy with a video camera.

"I'm from channel 9 and we'd like to interview both of you for the 5:00 evening news."

Ryan acts like this happens every day and I try to play along. I'm sticky and dirty, but all I really have to do is answer questions about the race, and my plans for the rest of the season. They ask

Ryan questions about his college choices, and he provides the names of a few schools he's looking at.

Jenny jogs up to me afterward. "Looks like you might get a chance to see yourself running after all. I heard they video taped the whole race."

Gran hears about the news interview and glues herself to the television as soon as we get home. She's bursting with pride, calling all of her friends to tell them to turn on the television. If nothing else, I'm thankful that Gran gets so much pleasure out of watching me run. I think if I placed last in every race, she'd be just as enthusiastic. She is impressed with my races no matter what the result.

The image on the screen flashes to the starting line of the Aspen Leaf Invitational before flashing to an image of me running as I break away from the rest of the girls.

"Brockton Public dominated the twenty-sixth Aspen Leaf Invitational this morning. Reigning state champion, Pepper Jones, cruised into the finish with a smile on her face, nearly thirty seconds ahead of second place finisher, Kendra Smith."

I hardly recognize myself when the screen zooms in on me running towards the finish line. Jenny was right. If it wasn't for the uniform and the cheering fans, you wouldn't know I was racing. Like Ryan, I look relaxed. My legs float along the grass, propelling me forward with seemingly effortless momentum. When the screen flashes to other finishers, the contrast is unnerving. Their arms are pumping hard, and their faces are twisted from the exertion.

After reviewing the boys' race, the commentator shows clips from the interview with me and Ryan. "Today's wins for Harding and Jones are just the beginning. We'll be watching these two young athletes when they take on the national field."

When?

After seeing myself cross the finish line, I find myself believing that the television commentator might just know what he's talking about.

Chapter 12

When I step out of my last class of the day the following Monday, Ryan is waiting for me. His sandy brown hair is tousled, like he's been running his hands through it.

"Hey," Ryan puts his arm around my shoulder and I lean into him. It feels good. I've become really comfortable with him in such a quick period of time. "You have study hall next, right?" He asks.

"How'd you know?" I glance at him curiously.

"I've seen you leaving the library after this period before. I have photography across the hall. We just have to check in today and then we're supposed to leave the classroom to take photos. Wanna hang out?"

I put my hand over my mouth in mock horror. "And skip study hall?"

Ryan smiles, displaying his matching dimples. "I didn't say that. We could hang out in the library. But if you want to skip, I have some ideas."

"There really is no such thing as skipping study hall, Ryan. Nobody checks you in. It's just a chance to get homework done so you don't have to do it later," I tell him.

"Yeah, I figured that out pretty quickly when I showed up in the library for my first study hall and no one else was there. But you always go," he points out.

I shrug. "I don't have a car to go anywhere so I figure I might as well get my homework done with the free time."

"So, you're up for an adventure then?" He smiles encouragingly.

I glance at my watch. "We only have an hour before practice. How much of an adventure can we fit in before that?"

"Grab your running stuff. We'll change and meet by my car."

Curious, I follow his instructions and head out to the senior parking lot. It's an unseasonably warm day for early October. It must be in the eighties. Last week it seemed like summer was over, but today the sun is beating strong. I hope it's the last hot day of the year, because I prefer to race in cold temperatures. I put on my sunglasses and look around for Ryan's car. He's leaning against it in the far corner and waving at me.

"So, I actually learned about this spot I want to take you to from Kevin," he says when I reach him.

"Your little brother? He's in eighth grade, right? He was really cute but I didn't really get a chance to talk to him at the meet."

"Cute, huh? Don't tell him that. He has not stopped asking about you," Ryan says with a chuckle. "Kev's totally crushing on you. Wants to come to all our meets. He'll probably bring his little buddies so he can show them how hot you are. But I think the eighth grade boys already know. You're like a local celebrity, you know?" Ryan opens the passenger side door and I hop in.

I roll my eyes. "I think maybe Kevin is exaggerating because he's a runner too. We runners like to think people pay more attention to running than they do."

A few minutes later, Ryan turns on to Hidden Falls Lane. "You aren't afraid of heights, are you?" He asks me.

"Nope. But I know where you're taking me. It's not exactly a huge secret."

"Well, shoot. You could've at least pretended to be impressed," Ryan teases.

Hidden Falls is a series of swimming holes that pool along the river. There are rocks you can jump off into the holes. "Actually, I've only been here once before," I admit. "And I only jumped from one of the little rocks. Maybe I'll try the thirty footer today."

We pull up along the road behind a couple of other parked cars. Ryan tosses me a towel from the backseat. "You're prepared," I say, impressed. "Did you know we were going to do this?"

Ryan smiles sheepishly. "Actually, I was thinking of taking you by here after practice. I checked the weather and saw how hot it was going be and thought we might want to cool off after practice. But beforehand is just as good."

"You didn't tell me to bring a bathing suit," I point out. We head down the path towards

"You can just go in your shorts and sports bra right? You'll dry off super quick." We hear yelling and laughing as we approach the river. "Sorry, I didn't think anyone would be around. You know, you run in your sports bra and stuff so I hope it's okay. . ." Ryan drifts off.

I laugh. "It's fine, Ry. Shorts and a sports bra are far less revealing than a bathing suit anyway."

Ryan takes my hand and pulls me closer to him.

"You called me Ry," he says with a grin.

I lift my finger to touch one of his dimples and shrug. "It just slipped out."

"I like it." He lowers his forehead to mine and I think he's going to kiss me. Instead, he just rests his head against mine for a minute. "You're gorgeous, Pepper, you know that?"

I raise my eyebrows. "Ummm..." That is not something *friends* tell each other.

We continue walking towards the falls, hand in hand. My steps falter when I see Madeline standing on the edge of the thirty footer looking down. Speaking of gorgeous. She's wearing a purple string bikini and her hand is on her hip. Unlike my shorts tan line, she is evenly tanned all over, without a single blemish. She turns her head in our direction when she hears us walking towards her.

I feel Ryan hold my hand tighter as Madeline's eyes drift down to our locked hands. She watches us curiously as we approach. "Hi, Ryan." Madeline steps towards us and I hate the way she blatantly checks him out. Ryan's only wearing his running shorts and flip-flops. He's not jaw-dropping Jace Wilder, but he's definitely hot, no doubt about it.

"Hi, Madeline," he says.

I'm relieved he hasn't completely lost it and turned into a panting teenage boy. I imagine most boys get that way around Madeline, and I can tell she's a little put off by his lack of reaction. She is wearing a bikini, after all. But Ryan keeps his eyes on hers, even though I have no doubt they want to drift down.

She glances at me. "Pepper, hello. Does Jace know you're skipping class?"

I narrow my eyes. It's a dig at me, and she knows it. She's trying to insinuate that Jace treats me like a kid, and she wants Ryan to know that Jace can control who I hang out with and when.

"No, Madeline. Jace doesn't need to know everything I do. And I'm not skipping. I have a free period." So it's a half lie. Whatever.

I must have become her enemy at some point and I'm not sure how that happened. Madeline purses her lips. "He likes to keep tabs on you. I'll let him know tonight. He's taking me out to dinner."

Jace doesn't take girls on dates; everyone knows that. She's either lying or Jace is up to something.

"Madeline! What are you doing? Get down here!" Emma yells from the swimming hole below. Madeline turns to the edge. She plugs her nose before jumping off. We hear her screeches before she falls into the water.

I turn to Ryan, who is watching me. He brushes a loose hair from my forehead. Only Jace has done that before, and I'm not sure how I feel about someone else doing it. "I can tell Madeline isn't the nicest person. We don't have to stick around," he offers.

"No way. I'm not leaving just because she's here. Let's jump!" I toss my tee shirt and towel by a tree and kick off my flip- flops. I walk to the edge and peek over. I can see Emma and Serena lounging on a flat rock. I recognize Wesley's blonde hair as he swims by Madeline. Pierce and Forbes are climbing along the side of a rock, showing off for the girls.

Wes glances up my way when he sees Emma and Serena looking my direction. His eyes dart to Ryan, who is standing behind me.

"What do you think?" Ryan asks.

"About jumping? I'm going for it. But if I stand here any longer I'll psych myself out." I glance down one more time to make sure Wes and Madeline are out of the landing zone before I leap off.

The warm air rushes past me and my heart drops to my belly as the world flashes by. I point my toes in anticipation and feel the cold water crash around me. My body drops below the surface and I wait to see how far I will sink. All I can see are white bubbles around me. My toes never touch the bottom before I start kicking to the surface. When my head pops up, Wes is treading water right by me. He sees my grin and smiles with relief.

"How'd that feel?" he asks.

"That was awesome! I'm going again!" I swim to the side and look up at Ryan, who's standing on the edge. "Go for it!" I yell.

He jumps forward and flips in a somersault before landing. Show off. Wes glances over at me. It looks like he wants to say something but he keeps his mouth closed. Ryan and I scramble back up and jump off a couple more times. I lie out on a rock a little ways from the pool to try to dry off before we get in his car. Ryan lies down next to me.

"Thanks for bringing me," I tell him.

We lie on our backs, eyes closed, enjoying the warmth of the sun. I sense a shadow over me and feel cold water drip onto my belly. I open my eyes. Madeline is standing over me.

"Pepper, I want to ask you about something," she tells me.

"Yeah?" I ask. "What is it?"

"Let's walk together," she says it like a command, not a request.

"Okaaay," I say skeptically.

We walk along the path, away from the swimming hole.

"So, I was wondering what's going on with Pierce and your friend who came to the party at Wes's place."

I shrug. I hardly know this girl. Why is it any of her business? "Nothing's going on as far as I know."

She crosses her arms. "See, that's the thing. I know you probably don't think this is any of my business but I'm asking for Pierce. He's my friend. He really likes Zoe and thought she liked him, too. Didn't it seem that way to you at Wes's place?"

"Yeah," I concede.

"So now she doesn't want to see him again. There must be some explanation."

I sigh. Maybe if I give her some information she'll give me some. "Zoe's dad's a cop." I wait to see any reaction from Madeline. Her eyebrows raise infinitesimally. "He just told Zoe that he wasn't happy with her hanging out at Wes's house, or dating Wes's friends. He thinks they, or you, maybe, I don't know, are bad kids or something."

I watch Madeline purse her lips as she mulls this information over. "Did he say why?"

"No, but Zoe heard him talking to her mom later about Wes being involved with drug dealing. Do you know anything about that?"

Madeline shakes her head back and forth slowly, but I sense she wants to tell me something. "Why would Wes deal drugs?" I ask. "He's loaded."

Madeline cocks her head to the side. "What else do you think people get out of dealing drugs beside money?"

I raise my hands. "Besides drugs? I wouldn't know."

"If you already have money you can just buy drugs if that's all you want. Think about it, Pepper."

"Maybe some sort of authority, or control or power or something. Madeline, I don't know anything about that stuff, seriously."

"I don't know, seems like you have the idea to me."

"What are you saying? Wes deals drugs for power and control? He doesn't need that either." I cross my arms. What's the point of this conversation? What's Madeline's want from me?

"Look, I know you don't go out much, but you know the way it is. Think about Wes. He seems to have it all. But then think about Jace, right?"

"So it's some kind of rivalry," I say slowly. And Jace is involved.

Madeline watches me. "Come on, Pepper. You're a smart girl. Maybe being the shit at Lincoln isn't enough for Wes. It's a smaller school. And Brockton's a big town. There's more than just high school."

I think about Jace, his college friends, and his strange alliance with Wesley. "I have to go." I turn away and tell Ryan we should head back.

Jace doesn't show up for dinner after practice. As soon as I'm done eating, I head over to the Wilders' house and walk through the front door without knocking. I see Jim in the kitchen getting a beer and I wave as I jog down the stairs.

When I burst through Jace's bedroom door, he's standing in front of his closet in nothing but black boxer briefs and socks. Shit. He looks far too good and it's incredibly distracting. My gaze lingers on the muscular curve of his bottom for a moment before I plop myself on his bed and cross my arms.

"Alright, buddy. I want answers. Now."

Jace watches me carefully. "What's going on, Pep?" he says quietly.

I point my finger at him. "Don't even pretend to act like you don't know what I'm talking about."

Jace sits on the very edge of his bed, as far from me as possible. He rubs his hands over his face.

"What do you want to know?"

"Are you dealing drugs?"

"Yeah, a little," he says slowly. "But don't worry Pep, it's not that big of a deal."

"Not that big of a deal? Jace, I've never given you a hard time about stuff you do, but this? It's just stupid. Why would you risk a football scholarship?" That's not the only question I have, but it's a starting point. And it should get his attention.

Jace shrugs. "It's just some easy money on the side, Pep. I'm training for football all the time. I don't have time for a real job."

I just stare at him. He has to know how stupid he sounds.

Jace leans back on his elbows and my eyes go straight to his abs. "Look Pep, this is one of the reasons I keep you at a distance. You don't need to be a part of this."

I ignore that statement, for the time being, and ask another question. "And Wes? What does he have to do with it?"

"He got himself into a little trouble dealing last year, and I helped smooth things over. That's how I got into it in the first place. Now, it's just easy cash. I know the guys I'm dealing with, and it's a pretty straight forward thing we have going on."

"What do you mean he got himself into some trouble?" I swirl my bracelets around my wrist as I process the information.

"The guy he was buying from was picked up, and Wes thought his name was going to get dropped. He called me to make sure it didn't."

"Huh?"

"Nevermind. Wes and I hadn't been close for awhile, but that doesn't mean I wanted him to get fucked over."

That part, I get. The rest of the details, I'm not exactly following. I suppose they aren't so important. "You told me not so long ago that you didn't do drugs. Were you lying?"

Jace runs his hand through his hair again. He stands up and paces around the room. It's impossible to focus on anything else but his half naked body. Why can't he throw some clothes on, for goodness sake?

"No, not really. I tried some shit a few times, but I hadn't done much in a while when I told you that. Recently, well... I've been partying a little more than usual." Jace looks away when he says this and I can tell there's more behind that statement.

I shake my head, unable to process this information. In some ways, it rips me up that there's this whole side of Jace I knew nothing about. But on the other hand, I know this isn't all that out of character for him. Jace has always been all about power and control. Even as a little kid. He's always had it, and this is another way to hold onto it.

Jace's phone rings from the bedside table and I glance at it. Madeline. Of course, they had a date tonight.

"Just a sec," he murmurs before answering.

"Seriously?" I ask, trying to hold back any emotion. We're in the middle of an important conversation, and he cuts it off to talk to his fuck buddy? Until now, I thought I came before the girls he slept with. Did that change when I kissed him?

"Hey," he says in the phone. I can hear her muffled voice on the other line.

I don't stick around to listen.

Chapter 13

Things aren't the same with Jace after I confront him. After we kissed, we could at least *pretend* like things hadn't changed. Sort of. Temporarily, at least.

But now, I feel like I don't understand him anymore. This time, his controlling nature doesn't explain his actions – instead, it's like he's out of control. Orgies, regular drug use, dealing. . . it's too much.

I know Jace, and if he decided to deal, he's not bothering with small bags of pot. I don't doubt for a minute he moved right into more serious stuff. Brockton's a college town, and there's plenty of partying. CU's known for it. His unexplained absences from dinners, the out of town trips, and the college friends - it makes sense now. He's got a whole little secret life that I am not a part of. And I don't want to be.

Our morning car rides are awkward. I simply can't relax and be myself with him anymore. He knows it too. We don't bother pretending. Jace doesn't make it to dinner all week, and I decide to arrange rides with Ryan in the morning, telling Jace he doesn't need to pick me up.

I've always known Jace and I were different. I like to play it safe. I have just what I need with running, my few friends, Gran, and Dave. I could accept that Jace had his own little world that wasn't for me. Until now.

I know it's time to snap out of it when the district meet arrives at the end of October. My equilibrium has definitely shifted with the absence of Jace in my life, but there's no reason it should impact my running.

We meet in the school parking lot at seven the morning of the race to take the bus as a team. When I step on, I see that Zoe is already sitting with Charlie. They look quite cozy. I scan through my memories of the last week and realize that they have definitely been acting differently towards each other. Hmmm. . .

Taking a seat near the back, I slip on my headphones and prop up my pillow, hoping to remain anti-social for as long as possible. I close my eyes and snuggle against the window.

When the bus starts to move I feel someone sit in the seat next to me. A shoulder brushes mine. I pull out my headphones and look at the intruder. Ryan is leaning his head to the side looking at me. "Hi," he says.

"Did the headphones, closed eyes and pillow not send the right message?" I tease.

"Sorry. I was sitting near the front, but I saw you way back here and wanted to see what was up. You feel okay?"

I'm not usually anti-social like this so I suppose it does cause suspicion. "Yeah, Ryan, I'm good. Thanks though."

He watches me for a moment, unsure whether to leave or not. "So, you ready for the first meet in our championship season?" I ask, encouraging him to stay.

He smiles. "Yeah, I guess so. You've done this course before, right?"

I start telling him about the course. Last year, we had an early season dual meet on the District course. I was in the lead and took a wrong turn. "Hopefully it'll be better marked than it was for the deal meet. But I'd pay attention during the walk through just in case. There are lots of sneaky turns!"

Ryan laughs and tells me that the same thing happened to him once but he was able to back track without losing the lead.
I watch him as he talks. His sandy brown hair is long enough to tuck behind his ears. The shaggy look is endearing. Ryan is

classically good looking in a boyish way. He's even cuter when he smiles, which he's doing a lot while he talks. I find myself leaning closer towards him. The hard layer I've been wearing the past couple of weeks starts to soften a little. I feel, I don't know, *warmer*, in his presence.

The next thing I know, Ryan is shaking me gently. I blink my eyes open, and find my head is resting on his chest. I whip my head up, thankful there's no drool running from my mouth. "Sorry!" I exclaim.

"We're here," he tells me. I look out the window. Several other school busses are parked around us and groggy teenagers are wandering around in shorts and sweatshirts.

"Whoa. Guess I was tired. Sorry about that."

"Don't worry about it," Ryan reaches out and squeezes my shoulder.

During warm-up, I ask Zoe about Charlie. "Finally!" she answers. "I was wondering when you were going to get with the program!"

"Sorry. I've been in my own head lately," I admit.

"We kind of got together last weekend," Zoe tells me.

Apparently he was helping her study for AP bio and then he asked her to stay to watch a movie, and one thing led to another, and they crossed the line from friends to friends who make out. Now they apparently cuddle in public too.

"He's taking me on a real date after the meet. I think we're just going to dinner or something. But it's kind of weird changing my mindset." My mind immediately jumps to the changes happening between Jace and me . . . and Ryan and me. "It's like I must have had these feeling buried for him and now that I'm not suppressing them I think of him totally differently. I'm not sure how we kept it platonic for so long!" *Platonic.* I hate that word.

We're heading over the last hill of the course, finishing our warm up, when I see Brockton Public's junior varsity football team running at us. Shirtless. And covered in blue paint. They have letters painted on their chests and are screaming and cheering.

"Do they know that we're just warming up?" Jenny asks.

We gape as they swarm around us, jumping in the air. How do they have so much energy? "Red Bull," Zoe answers my unasked question.

The guys start organizing themselves in two lines and we can make out what the letters on the chests spell. One line says "Brockton" and the other says "Pepper." It's quite impressive. And I know who organized it. Jace is at a college visit in Michigan this weekend, but only he would be able to get fifteen high school boys to cheer at a cross meet first thing on a Saturday morning.

As we jog back to the team tent, I see Gran standing on the sideline by her chair snapping photos of the football team running beside us. She's by Zoe and Claire's parents, and some other parental types who look familiar. I wave and she gives a double thumbs up and a toothy grin. She's decked out in our school color, royal blue, from head to toe. She's even got a blue winter hat and blue high top Nikes.

It's a cold morning and I can see my breath. I wear a long sleeved shirt underneath my singlet, a blue headband that covers my ears, and gloves. Hopefully the shirtless fans won't get hypothermia.

We huddle in a circle with our arms over each other's backs. Claire's my co-captain and she usually leaves it to me to give a pep talk before our team cheer. She surprises us when she speaks up.

"I'm not running in college so this could be my last cross meet. I hope it won't be, because I know that we can qualify for State as a team. I just want to tell you all that being on this team has been my favorite part of high school. So, thanks. Anyway, I hope you guys all run your hearts out today because I really want my last meet to be the State championship."

We just barely missed making State as a team last year, and Claire missed making it individually by two spots. If there's anyone to dig deep for today, it's her. And I think even Dorothy knows it.

We scream our cheer and jog to the start line. Because there are so many teams, only two of us can toe the line. Claire is next to me, Chloe and Jenny are in the row behind us, and Dorothy with our two other varsity runners are behind them. It's going to be a messy start with all these girls.

"Runners, take your mark . . ." BOOM! The gun goes off and I sprint forward to get away from the crowd. Normally I wouldn't go out this hard but it beats getting trampled. The sound of the fans cheering is a blur as I keep my elbows to the side to prevent getting knocked over.

The crowd quickly thins out and the path narrows before entering the woods. Settling in with a pack of about ten others, I take stock and recognize all of the runners from other meets. There are three or four who could give me a good race, including Kendra Smith who placed second at the Aspen Leaf Invitational. But I'm feeling fairly confident that I've got this.

Coach Tom is standing at the top of the first hill. "Settle in, Pepper! You look great. Stay right there!" The plan's to run in the lead group until the top of the last hill, about 800 meters from the finish. No matter how good I feel, I'm supposed to stay with them. Coach thinks 800 meters is plenty safe to allow me to break away, since I've got a decent kick.

I focus on staying behind the three girls in front of the pack who are setting the pace. Following someone else's lead isn't in my nature, and it's hard to suppress the urge to burst through them and take off.

One of the shirtless entourages is lined up along the side of a straightaway when we come out of woods towards the end of the first mile of the 3.1 mile (5 kilometer) race. They scream and cheer while running alongside us for about 100 meters before slowing to a stop. We're running close to a 5:30 pace so keeping up for more than 100 meters isn't exactly easy, all things considered. I smile at the guys, and I almost wave, before realizing it would be sort of an insulting demonstration of my lack of effort to the other runners who aren't holding anything back.

We're about halfway through the race when we pass by the starting line and a roar of cheers. There are fans scattered throughout the course, but most people have congregated by the start/finish area. I see Gran bouncing up and down in her bright blue outfit and I grin at her.

"Go, Pepper, go!" She screams.

A couple of girls start dropping back until there are only five of us in the lead pack. Coach Tom is at the edge of the field when we reenter the woods for our final loop. He must sense my impatience because he yells, "Keep it steady, Pepper. Right at this pace."

Watching the ponytail of the girl in front of me sway back and forth, I try to relax. But my legs are itching to go faster. The cold air is refreshing, and the fans' energy is contagious.

When we pass by the 2-mile marker, I find myself moving in front of the other four girls. I don't consciously decide to drop them. Maybe they just slowed down. But once I see that there is no one beside me or in front of me, I drop the hammer.

I fly up the last hill, which has always felt like a steep mountain when I've raced this course before. I hardly notice the boys' team cheering for me at the top of the hill. I've never been high, but I'm pretty sure it must feel something like this. It's like my body has just taken over and I can't be stopped. I keep going faster, and the slight burn in my chest and ache in my legs only drives me to push harder.

I accelerate down the hill and into the large field, where hundreds of people are on their feet cheering. The finish line is just ahead, and the clock above it with the ticking time is a blur. It doesn't even matter what my time is. This feeling alone is amazing.

I burst through the finish line with a huge grin on my face. I can hear the announcer. "Pepper Jones is the district champion. And in a new course record of 16:48, ladies and gentlemen . . ."

It's my fastest time ever, and not just on this course. I've never run a 5 kilometer cross country course in under 17 minutes before.

I make my way out of the finish area so I can cheer for the rest of the team. Claire and Zoe are racing right next to each other and I cheer like a maniac when they run by me. They cross the finish at the same time, and I watch them give each other an exhausted hug before collapsing to the ground.

"Pepper!" Ryan runs towards me and lifts me up in the air to twirl me around. "That was incredible!"

I laugh. "Hey! Put me down, you need to conserve your energy!"

"I don't care. I'm inspired. That was the most badass run ever."

When he lets me go, Charlie scoops me up for another hug that lifts me off the ground. "I'm proud of you, Pepper."

After the boys race, we find out that both the girls' and the boys' team won Districts, claiming the individual and team titles. Rollie invites everyone over to his house to celebrate. The runners who aren't on varsity come as well, and there must be at least fifty people crowded into the den in his basement.

The party is almost as big as the one at Remy's house, but instead of feeling out of place, I'm surrounded by all my friends. And we definitely don't need any alcohol to lift our spirits. The relatively tame pizza party quickly turns into a crazy dance party.

with some of the quietist members of the team dancing on the coffee table and jumping on the couch. It could simply be a sugar high from drinking soda, but Brockton's cross team is in wild form. A great race will do that to runners.

Ryan is standing talking to Omar and Rollie when one of my favorite Justin Timberlake songs starts playing. I grab his hands and pull him towards me. I start dancing playfully around him until he has no other choice but to join me. He's a good dancer, but keeps it simple, letting me be the one to really move. I love to dance, but it's usually just with Zoe or Gran. Dancing with a boy, especially a cute one like Ryan, is exhilarating.

He seems to appreciate my enthusiasm, and pulls me in closer to him. Before I know it, I'm pressed up so close to Ryan that my swaying hips seem inappropriate with an audience. We are chest to chest, and with my arms wrapped around his neck, I can feel each hard angle of his body. I murmur the lyrics to the song and tone down my dancing so we're just shifting lightly together in sync with the beat.

We continue dancing together for several more songs, and its not until I realize people have started to head home that we break apart. The adrenaline rush from the race and dancing is starting to fade, and I can tell I'm going to crash from exhaustion at any moment.

Zoe offers me a ride home, but Ryan jumps in, saying I'm on his way. I watch him discreetly for a moment in the car. His forehead is damp with sweat from dancing, and his blue eyes look soft and sleepy from the long day. When he glances at me, and smiles, showing off those adorable dimples, he looks so happy. And it all seems so simple with him.

He likes me. I like him.

If it wasn't for Jace, there would be no question at all what direction things should go with Ryan and me. And what's stopping me now?

Ryan clears his throat. "I don't know if this sounds weird or not, but I'd love for you to come to brunch tomorrow with my family."

"Why would that be weird?" I ask.

"I don't know. You've become a really good friend, and I've gotten to know your Gran, so I thought it'd be nice for you to get to know my family a bit." He pauses, like he's going to say more, but thinks better of it.

"Yeah, that'd be cool. I've never met your dad and he could be my coach someday, so it'd be great to talk to him."

When I get home, I see I have two missed calls from Jace and a text message congratulating me for the race. I didn't bring my phone with me to Rollie's because the only people who would call were at the party. Or so I thought. Apparently Jace wants things to go back to normal again.

And normally, I'd call him back. But who know what he's doing. He's in Michigan, on a college visit, so I can only imagine the shenanigans he's up to. I'm done being hurt by Jace. I need a break.

Ryan picks me up at ten the next morning.

"So where are we going?" I ask him as I buckle in. Driving around in the passenger side of his jeep has become a regular thing.

"Have you been to Lucille's?" He asks.

"Yes! I love Lucille's! Have you been?"

Ryan laughs. "Yeah, we went whenever I visited last year. I've developed a sick obsession with their beignets." My mouth waters just thinking about the deep fried pastry. "Sunday brunch is kind of a thing we've done forever with my family."

Ryan doesn't tell me that it's his mom's birthday until after we've parked and we're walking to Lucille's. The wrapped gift he pulls out from behind the driver's seat gives it away. "This is a family thing, are you sure I'm invited? I didn't bring anything. I'm going to look like a jerk!"

Ryan takes my hand and kisses me on the cheek. It feels so natural, like we've been doing it for years. "She's thrilled you're coming. That's a present on its own."

I recognize the Harding family from a block away. Ryan's parents and younger brother are thin, fit, and good looking. That's not especially unusual in Brockton, but there's a wholesome, all-American quality about them that Ryan has too.

Ryan's mom beams when she sees us. "Pepper! It's so nice to see you again. We're really happy you could join us."

"Thanks Mrs. Harding. And happy birthday. Ryan just told me, so I didn't get a chance to bring anything." I elbow him playfully.

"Oh, no, you didn't need to bring a thing. And it's Marie, honey. Mrs. Harding is my mother-in-law. You remember Kevin, right?" She gestures to Ryan's little brother, who smiles shyly. "And this is my husband, Mark."

"Hi Mr. Harding, it's nice to meet you."

"Call me Mark, please." He laughs. Mark must be in his forties, but he still has the unmistakable physique of an elite runner. He was a professional marathoner for years, and I think won some major titles. Chicago or New York? Maybe both. I'll have to ask him about it.

"We should be up any minute. You know how it is here. There's always a wait," Marie says.

The Hardings ask about Gran, Dave, and growing up in Brockton. I feel like I'm talking their ears off, but they seem genuinely curious about what I have to say. When our name is called, we're placed at a table by the window, where we all have to sit very close together to fit. After ordering, Ryan gives Marie her present.

"She'll get the rest tonight, but I always give her one in the morning," Ryan explains.

"Ever since he was a little boy, he could never wait to give me my birthday present." Marie smiles lovingly at Ryan.

Marie unwraps the paper and pulls out a necklace with a turquoise pendant and matching earrings. The jewelry is both beautiful and trendy, and it suits her. I raise my eyebrows at Ryan. "You have good taste."

He shrugs and smiles. Mark helps her with the clasp and we all admire it. "Thanks, hun. You're so sweet." Marie leans across the table to kiss Ryan on the cheek.

For some reason, I leave the brunch feeling a little sad. Ryan's family is so normal. Two loving parents, and a sibling. I never had that. Jace never had that. I guess I never felt much of a longing for it either. My parents died when I was too little to remember, and all I've ever known of my family is Gran. And with Jace, he and his dad sort of filled in the empty spots. Jace didn't have a whole family either, and Wes's parents were always out of town growing up. Seeing Ryan's family like that, it just makes me feel like I missed out on something.

Gran's hanging out with Lulu, so I expect to come home to an empty apartment. Instead, Jace is sitting at the kitchen table. He looks up from his phone when I open the door.

"Hey," I say. "I thought you were in Michigan."

Jace stands up. He's wearing a pair of old sweat pants and a hooded CU football sweatshirt that used to be Jim's in college. The soft, worn clothing looks comfortable and it makes me want to wrap my arms around him.

"I got back this morning. I heard about your race, Pep. I'm so proud of you." He opens his arms for a hug, and though I'm still mad at him, not to mention hurt and confused about our relationship, I can't help but walk into his arms. The feel of his soft clothing and hard body against mine is one of the best feelings in the world. Comfort and protection all wrapped up in one. But I can't give in.

I'm the first to pull away. "You look like you could use a nap. I got your messages, Jace. You didn't have to come over."

"I know, but I wanted to. What were you up to this morning?" He asks.

"I went to Lucille's with the Hardings," I say as I make my way to the couch. Dave jumps up beside me.

"Ryan's family?" Jace asks with a frown. He settles in on the other side of the couch.

"Yeah." I snuggle up to Dave, who is sniffing me thoroughly. I'm sure I smell like fried dough and bacon.

"I didn't know," Jace says. "Are you two serious now?"

I really don't want to get into this with Jace. Ryan and I haven't even talked about it yet. "I think we're just friends. But I feel like that might be changing."

Jace raises his green eyes to meet my brown ones. He tilts his head to the side. I realize what I've just said could apply to Jace as well. Except maybe we're changing from friends to not friends at all.

"Changing?" he asks.

"Jace, I'm not going to tell you everything that's going on in my life anymore when you keep so much from me." I watch Jace's composed expression crumble. "Sometimes I feel like you know every little thing about me, and I don't know you at all."

I recognize Jace's lost little boy look and it makes me want to apologize, but I don't. This isn't okay with me anymore. Whatever *this* is.

Jace pulls something out of his pocket and places it on the kitchen table. It's a friendship bracelet. Just like the one I made him for his first football state championship his freshman year. Except this one is purple and white and his is green and white. It's about an inch wide – thick enough that it's held together all these years. He's still wearing it. Once it's knotted, you can't take it on and off.

"Where'd you get that?" I ask.

"I made it."

"You made it? Really?" I can't hide my surprise. "How'd you figure it out? You never used to want to learn."

"I looked it up online, and went to the craft store to get the stuff. I did it on the plane. The people sitting next to me probably thought it was pretty weird that a teenage boy was making jewelry."

I smile at the image of him hovered over the strings, trying to braid them together without messing it up. "I'm impressed."

"Took me a few tries," Jace says with a gentle smile. "Want me to tie it on for you?"

I hesitate. Once it's on, I can't take it off without cutting it. And I'm not sure how I feel about having a reminder of Jace attached to me indefinitely. "Not yet."

Jace's smile fades and he stands up. Dave jumps off the bed, apparently displeased that his buddy isn't joining the snuggle session on the couch.

"Hey Jace, the cheerleaders you sent yesterday were awesome. Thanks." It's an effort to smooth over my harsh words, but Jace doesn't want it.

"Later, Pep. Good luck at State," he says as he heads out the door. He must not plan on seeing me again before the State meet if he's wishing me luck now.

I take the bracelet and place it in my sock drawer. I don't know how   long   it   will   stay   there.

Chapter 14

I'm a wreck the week leading up to State. It'd be nice to have Jace's soothing and reassuring presence around, but I'm not sure if his presence still has that effect on me anyway.

Everyone's heard about Brockton's amazing wins at Districts, and the news stations are talking about our chances at winning the State team titles. They think it's a forgone conclusion that Ryan and I will win the individual titles. Kids in school are actually paying attention to cross and all my teachers have congratulated me on Districts and wished me luck for State.

It was flattering for about two seconds. Now, every mention of State just makes me want to throw up. I've never felt this much anxiety in my life.

My muscles are tight all week at practice, and I know that Coach can tell. It's not fatigue or injury, like he was worried about, but the weight of people's expectations that have made running less than enjoyable. For once, I'm actually not looking forward to the meet.

The morning of the big day, Gran is dressed in her fan attire, looking like a giant blueberry. She's bouncing around the kitchen before she's even had her cup of coffee, listing off everything that I need.

"Gran, I've done this before. Calm down. You're making me nervous." I hate to rain on her parade, but I am so not feeling it right now.

"Sorry, hun. Here's your tea." She hands me a to-go mug of steaming hot Earl Grey. I know she's added a drop of milk and excessive amounts of honey. I don't usually drink caffeine, but I started drinking tea before races when some of them required getting up at the crack of dawn, and now it's become a ritual.

Gran blasts a pump-up mix CD, courtesy of Zoe Burton, on our way to the meet. It's only a forty-five minute drive, and everyone's parents go to State, so we don't have to ride the bus as a team.

The familiar nervousness rumbles through me when we pull up into the large field to park. The butterflies in my stomach are actually kind of comforting, because I always get them before I race. I breathe in deeply, trying to tell myself that this is just like any other meet. But I know it's a lie. If I don't place in the top seven, my season is over. I won't go on to Regionals, and definitely not Nationals. Not to mention that the team is counting on me to win for a chance at the team title.

Gran turns up the volume, moving her head up and down to the beat of Eminem. I smile to myself, knowing that she's sensed my anxiety and is trying to distract me with her ridiculousness. After we park, I kiss Gran goodbye while she pulls her camping chair and a huge blanket out of the trunk.

"Go get 'em!" She raises her fist in the air and I laugh, shaking my head.

We're quieter than usual during warm up, and I know we're feeling the pressure of winning a State championship. There's not much to say to ease the tension.

When we jog by other teams, I get that prickly feeling when you know people are starting at you. It doesn't help my queasy stomach. This local celebrity status thing isn't for me.

The State course is fast. There are hardly any hills, and most of the fastest times in the high school record books are recorded on the course. If I ran a 16:48 at Districts, who knows how fast I can run at State this year? Maybe I'll even break the twenty-year old State record. That's what everyone else has been talking about at least. But my time doesn't matter. First place does.

When the gun goes off, I sprint towards the front of the pack, just like I did at Districts. I can tell immediately that this isn't going to be my best race. Getting to the front of the pack shouldn't be a huge undertaking, but my heart is racing and my legs feel tight.

I settle in with the front group, recognizing most of the girls from other races. Just stick with them, I tell myself. Easy peasy, right? Usually I have to hold back in order to stick with the lead pack. Today, my legs feel like bricks, and it's all I can do to hang on.

The crowd shouts over the steady breathing of the girls around me. I recognize our royal blue uniform from the corner of my eye and I'm surprised to see Jenny running beside me.

Shaking out my hands, I struggle to find a rhythm. I regulate my breathing, but the tension in my body won't dissipate. When we pass the first mile marker, it's hard to believe there are still two more miles to go. It's already the longest race of my life and I'm not even halfway done.

Suddenly, it's not just my legs that feel heavy and tight. My head starts to spin, and the moving bodies around me fade in and out. I blink in confusion, but it only causes black dots to dance around me. I feel bodies brush past me as I stumble, and the next thing I know, I'm lying on my back on the trail, looking up at a cloudy sky.

Footsteps pound all around me. "Pepper!" It's Coach Tom.

I sit up and look around. People on the sidelines are shouting, but girls continue to run past.

"Keep racing, girls. Keep going," an official shouts from the sideline.

A stranger is at my side, explaining she's a doctor, and asking me questions. I start to stand, and stumble. Coach tries to take my arm to lead me off the course.

My head is in a frenzy. I don't know what happened to me, but every instinct tells me I need to run. Fast. No holding back.

"Coach, I'm going to keep going," I announce.

Coach looks at the doctor, who immediately says that's a bad idea. I can see she's just a spectator, and she can't make me sit out the rest of the race. But Coach agrees with her. "Pepper, you don't have to. What happened? Are you okay?"

"I'm going Coach. I can't lose any more time." And with that, I take off.

Coach runs along the side of the course, following me. He doesn't say anything. He probably expects me to collapse and wants to be ready to pick up the pieces.

My legs no longer feel like bricks, and my head is clear. Falling to the ground must have broken the tension in my body because the sensation of running is familiar again.

Most of the field passed me when I fell, but I start to pick them off again as I move through the second mile. I have no idea what I expect to accomplish at this point, but I'm not giving up.

I pass Dorothy, who actually shouts encouragements when I run by her. Seeing Zoe's familiar strawberry blond hair ahead, I will myself to close in the gap. I might not make it back to the top seven, but I'll at least score points for the team.

I don't have the breath to say anything to Zoe when I pass her, but I hear Coach tell her to pick it up and try to catch the group ahead of us. "Follow Pepper!" He yells.

She tags on to my pace, and Coach continues to run along the sideline. The race directors wouldn't normally allow him to run the course with us like this, but he's out of the way, and I'm sure me passing out is a good enough reason for him to stay by me.

We catch the next group of girls, and I recognize Claire in the front of the pack.

"Work together girls!" Coach yells. He disappears from my peripheral vision.

Claire does a double take when I run up beside her. She must not have seen me on the ground when she passed me. I'm sure she's totally confused as to why I'm coming up from behind. I flash her a smile but I don't slow the pace. I'm running hard, and I continue right on past the pack.

Zoe's heavy breathing tells me she's still with me. I glance behind me and give Claire what I hope is an encouraging look. She picks up her pace and settles in by Zoe as we surge ahead.

I can't see far enough ahead on the windy trial to know how many people are still in front of us. We pass one girl after another. The sound of Zoe and Claire breathing behind me helps with the forward momentum. It's three of us now, and we charge ahead like an unstoppable force. People on the sidelines cheer louder when they see our matching uniforms.

We round the last corner before the final stretch. The last 400 meters are downhill. There's another familiar royal blue uniform ahead, and I recognize Jenny's tiny frame sprinting towards the finish.

The throbbing in my legs doesn't stop me as I pump my arms and propel myself forward. I'm not getting enough oxygen and it hurts to breath, but I'm getting closer to the finish line, and closing the gap to Jenny. I can't hear Zoe and Claire behind me anymore. The only sound that reaches me is screaming fans.

I watch Jenny push through the finish line and I'm seconds behind her. I stumble again, and the blurred vision from earlier returns. I feel arms wrap around me, and instead of collapsing to the ground, I'm knocked over by Zoe, followed by Claire and Jenny. We're a pile of limbs, hugging each other in what I assume is celebration.

An official gently asks us to move away from the finish line.

"What happened to you?" Jenny asks. "You were right there one second and gone the next!"

"I saw you lying on the ground and I was about to stop but Coach yelled for me to keep going!" Zoe exclaims.

My legs are weak when I stand, and I keep my arms around Zoe and Claire to steady myself.

"I think I fainted," I tell them. "I didn't really feel like myself for the first mile and then all of a sudden things got all blurry and boom! I was lying on the ground."

"I didn't even see you!" Claire says. "You just came running by me, and I looked up because your speed startled me. I didn't know what was going on but when I saw Zoe with you, I just figured I had to stick with you guys."

Coach jogs up to us when we get through the crowds. He can hardly believe that all four of us placed in the top twenty-five, earning all-state individual honors. "I can't imagine you didn't win the team title." I'm afraid to ask what place I got. "We don't know exactly where you all placed yet, but the unofficial results will be out in a minute."

Coach can't make eye contact with me, and I know he's worried that I wasn't in the top seven. My season might be over. But I can't be too disappointed if I helped us win a team State championship. And I helped in a way that matters even more than my individual point contribution – I helped pull along my teammates.

Claire, Zoe, Jenny, and now the three other varsity runners who've joined us, are bursting with excitement. It's hard not to join them, but I know that later, when I'm alone, I'll be crushed by my individual failure.

Coach returns from the officials' tent a few minutes later. He looks elated, for the most part, but he still can't make eye contact with me.

"Congratulations to the Brockton High State Champions!" he booms. Before we can rejoice, he continues, "unofficially, Jenny placed seventh, Pepper eighth, Zoe eleventh, Claire twelfth, Dorothy forty-second..." Coach continues to speak but I can't hear anything except the buzzing in my ears.

Eighth?

Eighth.

Eighth!

Not top seven. No Regionals. No Nationals. It's over.

Instead of celebrating, everyone on the team wraps me in a sympathy hug. Great. My ambitions have ruined the moment.

I'm amazed I haven't burst into tears. Instead, I feel numb with shock. All the patience, the waiting, the holding back, was for nothing.

"Coach, isn't it true that if one of the top seven doesn't go to Regionals, they offer the spot to the next place?" Jenny asks.

"Yes. Last year Pepper didn't go, and I believe another girl who placed in the top seven couldn't go either, and the eighth and ninth place finishers went to Regionals instead."

"I'm not going," Jenny says.

"No way, Jenny," I protest. "You are not doing that so I can go. Besides, at least wait to see if anyone else drops out from the top seven before you give up your spot."

"Pepper, I didn't train for it. I'm not going to make Nationals. I'm ready for the season to be over, like you were last year. I really want you to go. You deserve it way more than me."

Nobody speaks. I want to take her offer, and her rationale makes some sense. She had an awesome State meet, but her chances of qualifying her Nationals are low.

"She does have three more years," Zoe says quietly.

"Pepper, it doesn't matter if you accept it or not. I'm going to give up my spot," Jenny tells me. And with that, she marches off the officials' tent.

Chapter 15

There are YouTube videos of me collapsing at State. I've watched it several times already. I'm jogging along in the middle of a pack of girls when I start to weave back and forth. I continue trying to run, but I stumble, sway from side to side, and wham! I'm down. I lie there for a good thirty seconds or so before sitting up. In total, I probably lost a minute before I started running again. That's pretty hard to come back from in a race when the winning time was 17:45.

I cut myself off from reading the YouTube comments and other runner discussion forums, and instead focus on getting my homework done and staying healthy for Regionals in less than two weeks. I spoke with the school physician and he said I probably just fainted. *Just* fainted! Who does that? I'd never fainted before.

Coach thinks I put too much pressure on myself and that the collapse was mentally induced. He doesn't think anything is wrong with me physically, and I agree. This week, it's only been Ryan and me at practice, and, while I can't exactly keep up with *him*, I feel pretty good. I feel myself again.

I'm lying on my bed doing physics homework one night the week after State, when my cell phone rings. It's not a number I recognize. "Hello?"

"Pepper. Hi." It's Wesley.

"How'd you get my number? I got this cell phone after we were friends."

Wes sighs. "Look, Pepper, it sucks that we stopped being friends. I don't want to get into the reasons for it now. Maybe someday. I really want to talk to you. Can we meet up?"

"Tonight? It's 9:30." It's almost my self-imposed bedtime. Wes might go out on weeknights, but I don't. "What's this about?" I ask skeptically.

"Jace." That's all he says.

Aside from a short text on Saturday after the race, I haven't heard from Jace since he came by after Districts and dropped off the bracelet.

"I'll borrow Bunny's car and meet you at your house." I tell Gran I'm heading over to Wes's house. She looks like she wants to ask questions, because this is out of character for me, but she doesn't.

I pull the car into Wes's driveway. The house is mostly dark. The front door opens before I've reached it and Wes stands there in sweatpants and a tight fitting cotton tee shirt. I'm wearing the same outfit and I'm glad I grabbed a zip up hoodie on the way out because I forgot that I'm not wearing a bra.

"Thanks for coming, Pepper." He holds open the door. "Do you want anything to drink?"

"No, thanks."

"Let's go up to my room." I follow him up the stairs. I haven't been in his room in years. It's huge, and he has his own walk-in closet and attached bathroom. A flat screen TV is on the wall across from his bed and it's playing a college football game. Wes picks up a bottle of beer from his desk and takes a sip.

"So?" I cross my arms over my chest.

He gestures to an armchair and I take a seat. Wes hops onto his desk and puts his feet on the desk chair. "I'm worried about Jace."

My eyes widen. "*You're* worried about Jace. Isn't that ironic?"

Wes studies me. His jaw works back and forth. "At first, I thought maybe something was happening with you two," he says. "You looked cozy at my house a month or two ago. I thought maybe it ended and that's why he was acting crazy." Wes glances at my expression and amends, "Well, crazier than usual. But then I saw you and Ryan together. So maybe it's Ryan that has Jace all worked up." Wes shakes his head. "But now, now I wonder if it's something else altogether."

Wes pierces me with his blue eyes, studying my reaction. "Either way, it has to do with you. You're the only one that gets to him."

I swallow hard. That actually might be true. But it's not about me. It's about control. It always is.

"Let's not worry about the why for now." I echo Wes's comments from earlier about the abrupt end to our friendship. "I want to know what you mean that he's acting crazier. Jace isn't the kind of guy people worry about. So what's going on?"

Wes runs a hand through his blonde hair. "Look, Jace'll kill me if I get into it. Just, he's not himself. And it's not healthy. I want to know what's going on so I can try to fix it. Or help."

"Boy, this is ironic." I roll my eyes. "You two are something else. Your ideas about 'helping' each other," I air quote, "seem to get you both into more trouble. Maybe you should just stay out of it. Jace can handle his own problems. He always has."

Wes narrows his eyes and runs his finger along his bottom lip. It's so weird that he still has the same familiar mannerisms. "What did Jace tell you, Pepper?"

"That you dealt drugs and Jace jumped in to 'help' you," I air quote again with my fingers, "with some sort of trouble and now he's a drug dealer, too." Maybe I'm not supposed to tell Wes what I know, but Wes dragged me into this and, at one time in our lives, we were close.

Wes clenches his jaw and looks away. "I could have figured it out without Jace."

"I don't care, Wes. I don't like it. Any of it. Whatever reasons you or Jace use to make it sound okay, it's not. You both have so much going for you. I don't understand why you'd risk it all. It's stupid."

Wes nods thoughtfully. "I take it that's what you told Jace?"

"Yeah."

Wes hops down from his desk and starts pacing around his room. "Does he know about Ryan?"

"What about Ryan? Jace doesn't control my life, Wes, even if he likes to think he does."

"Yeah, well, that's the problem. Or part of it." Wes continues pacing before sitting on the edge of his bed. "You can't shut him out, Pepper."

I shoot to my feet and point my finger at him. "Don't you start telling me what I can and can't do."

Wes stands up and holds my pointed finger in his hands. "I'm sorry. I didn't mean it like that. It's just, if you don't want Jace to ruin his life, you need to be there for him."

"I am here for him. He knows that. I just can't hang out with him like everything's okay. Because it's not. It's not okay. I'm so angry with him." I refrain from stomping my foot like an angry child but my eyes start to burn with unshed tears.

"It's not the same. He needs you around. You ground him, Pepper. He might still be a little crazy. Knowing you are seeing that Ryan guy," Wes says in a dismissive tone. What's *his* problem with Ryan? "But he'll cope. He'll keep it under control. Cause right now, he's outta control. And it's not good, Pep."

"What do you mean?" I force out.

Wes keeps holding my finger between his hands. "I know you don't like it, but Jace is smart about the stuff we do. He's totally business. He knows how to handle the guys we work with," Wes pauses when I give him a doubtful look. "Occasionally he'll party a little, but he never parties too hard. He's managed to keep his focus on football. If he gets caught, or starts using the shit we're pushing through, he'll lose any chance with football." *Duh.* Tell me something I don't know. "And right now, he's not being smart about dealing with people. He's acting like a hothead."

"Jace is always a hothead, Wes."

"Well, yeah, true. But I mean, shit . . . I shouldn't be telling you this."

"When did it start?" I ask.

"I guess I noticed the first time he got all crazy was that night I saw you at Remy's place," Wes says.

"And by get all crazy you mean, get super fucked up right?" I know what Wes was trying to say. Time to stop beating around the bush and get to the point.

Wes's eyes widen. I don't curse much. But I'm pretty wound up.

"Yeah. It was coke that night. I only started hanging out with him again last year, after football season. He never gets real fucked up though. He'll chill, have some drinks, and stayed in control you know?"

I nod solemnly. "Oh. I know."

"Anyway, the dudes we work with, they trust him. At least, as much as you can trust with this shit, but Jace is acting different. And it's not going to be good if he keeps this up."

I don't really know what Wes is talking about exactly but it makes me feel queasy. "What do you want me to do?" I whisper.

"Just, hang out with him again. Do your thing. Whatever it is you guys do."

I stare blankly at Wes. He invited me over here past my bedtime to give this explanation about things I don't want to know about, and *that's* his solution?

"I really don't think it's going to help, Wes."

"It will." Wes pulls me in for a hug. I'm so angry with Wes for pulling Jace in, but I can tell he really cares about Jace too. I allow myself to relax in his arms. But then I pull away, suddenly skeptical. I'd almost forgotten that I don't know this Wesley. I frown at him.

"You're only doing this because if Jace fucks up, you're screwed too."

Wes looks stricken, and I instantly regret saying it. "What? You think I don't care if Jace throws his life away? I know we haven't been friends for a while, but I care about Jace. I care about you, too. That never changed."

"But I don't know you anymore, Wes. You started dealing drugs. The Wes I knew wasn't that dumb."

"Jace started dealing drugs too, Pepper. And Jace isn't dumb," Wes points out.

I clench my teeth. Good point. But that's exactly why I feel like I don't get Jace anymore.

"You don't have to believe me. You don't have to like it. I want to be friends with you again. I probably won't, because Jace is volatile right now and it will set him off." I frown at that statement. "But I do know that you can't abandon your friendship with him right now. If you care about him, be that rock for him, you know? As best you can."

Rock? I'm Jace's rock? That's a heavy burden.

"Fine. But I'm watching you, Wesley Jamison." I point my finger at him. Wes grins and I can't help it when my lips lift into a small smile.

"Now, are you going to come with me to pick him up?" Wes asks.

"Pick him up? Right now?"

"Yeah, he's at Madeline's house."

"Uh, why does he need to be picked up?" I do not want to interrupt something. Definitely not.

"Emma and Serena are there too. They're rolling. He's been doing it a lot lately and it's gotta stop. That stuff is not meant to be used regularly. It's a party drug. For occasional use." Thanks for the information. Why do you sell it to people who can abuse it then? I want to ask.

"Maybe it's not supposed to be used ever," I say angrily. "What's rolling mean, anyway?"

"Ecstasy. He's taking ecstasy. At least, I was under the impression that's what was going down tonight," Wes says as he zips up a fleece.

"Why in the world would he leave if we show up?" If he's at one of those sex parties with three hot girls all over him I want nothing to do with it.

"He needs to know you care. That you're worried about him." I raise my eyebrows. Jace knows this already. He's known it his whole life. Wes continues, "If I bring you there, and say you came to me worried, he'll be pissed at me, but it'll hit home that what he's doing is wrong. He needs to see how you feel about it."

"Wes- he *knows* . . ." I start to explain, but Wes cuts me off.

"Yeah, he knows how you feel about it, but he won't change unless he really knows, you know?"

Maybe. Disapproving of his actions while we sit comfortably in his bedroom certainly isn't the same thing as interrupting it while it's happening. But I'm not entirely convinced.

"Whatever, Wes. This is a really dumb idea. You want him to see me angry?"

And hurt. I don't need to say it. Wes probably knows how I feel about Jace. If others can see it, there's no way it's escaped Wes. He knows this is going to hurt me.

"I'm waiting in the car," I tell him. "I'll call him. If he doesn't answer, you can go in and get him."

"Fine. Then just bring him home okay?" Wes says as we head down the stairs.

"If he comes out. What if he's in the middle of, you know?" I grimace.

I kind of hope Wes will deny that Jace might be doing "you know" with the girls, but he doesn't. "He'll come."

We look at each other, both realizing what he said at the same time. Despite the bizarre situation, I can't help the burst of laughter that erupts. It's silly, really, but somehow all the emotions built up inside of me come out in a fit of giggles. Wes joins me.

"He'll come. Oh Wes, that was good." I clutch my stomach and sigh. It really wasn't that funny, but I feel better.

Madeline lives a couple of streets down from Wes. "You weren't invited, huh?" I tease him as we pull up.

Wes doesn't respond and I glance over at him. His mouth is drawn in that tight, determined look. Maybe that was the wrong thing to ask. Maybe he wanted to be invited. Maybe he's making me come because he wants to be in Jace's shoes. What teenage boy wouldn't? Besides, these are Lincoln girls. It should be Wes, not Jace, who gets to sleep with them. He probably already has, but maybe not all in one night. How does a foursome work anyway? I shake my head, trying to clear it. It doesn't matter. I'll never need to know.

"Are you going to call him?" Wes asks.

I take out my phone and hit his number on speed dial. It rings several times and I'm about to hang up when a girl answers with a giggle. "Hellooooo?"

It sounds like Serena. At least it's not Madeline. "Hi. Is Jace there, please?"

"He's uh, indisposed, at the moment." I hear background noises that make me cringe. I might be sick. I can't believe Wes talked me into this.

"Who is it?" I hear Jace call.

"Don't worry about it, Jace. It's not important." She calls back. "Would you like me to pass any messages along?" She asks me.

"Just tell him that Pepper called, please." I know she knows it's me. My picture comes up on his phone when I call him.

"Okay." She hangs up.

I look at Wes. "Serena answered."

Wes leans his head back against the seat. "This isn't going to be fun. He might kill me. You sure you don't want to come to the door with me? It might save my life."

"Oh, please." I know he's kidding, sort of. "Just tell him I'm in the car before he can say anything. Then he'll at least be curious enough to wait for you to explain." I sigh before adding, "You know, I can just talk to him about all of this tomorrow. Do we really need to do it right now?"

"It'll be the most effective this way," Wes says as he gets out of the car.

I wait nervously, glancing at the clock at least a hundred times. Only eight minutes have gone by but it feels like hours. Finally, I see the front door open and Jace walks out with Wes. He looks relaxed and calm, not at all what I expected. It must be the drugs.

He slides into the passenger seat and Wes gets in the back seat. Jace gazes at me, his pupils dilated like I've never seen before. "Pepper," he says. It's a caress, and his voice is raspy. He's looking at me with desire.

"Jace," I say back, trying to sound serious. I haven't looked at him this closely in weeks, and I realize that I missed him more than I admitted to myself. We continue staring at each other, locked in some sort of weird staring contest, until Wes clears his throat.

"Guys? Let's go."

I turn on the car with shaky hands and drop Wes off at his house. Jace doesn't say anything, and every time I glance over he's staring at me. "Stop being a creeper, Jace."

"Sorry. You're just so beautiful, Pepper." I give him a doubtful look. Jace is fucked up right now so I can't really believe anything he says.

I'm supposed to be angry or hurt, and I think those feeling are buried in me somewhere, but the overwhelming emotion I feel is desire. Lust. He really needs to get out of the car. And I don't think Jace is feeling anything like remorse or regret, if the way he is looking at me is any indication. So much for Wes's plan.

"Can we have a sleepover tonight?" Jace asks when we pull into his driveway. "We haven't done one of those in forever."

We hadn't done one of those since Jace started high school. "I'm not going to sleep with you, Jace." I put the car in park and face him.

Jace reaches out and holds my hand, rubbing circles on the palm. "I don't mean sleep like that. I mean actually sleep. I've missed you so much." He watches our hands as he continues rubbing circles. "I won't be able to fall asleep in my bed. I just want to hold you." His voice is soft, and he sounds so lost. How can I possibly deny him? But this isn't right. Something is happening between Ryan and me and a sleepover with Jace is totally inappropriate.

"We can't, Jace. It's not right." Jace's hopeful expression crumbles. He drops my hand and looks down. He looks so sad. I feel guilty. After all, I did ruin his night.

"Wes said you were worried about me," he says.

"Let's not talk about that right now. I do worry. But I just want you home and safe and not messing around with a bunch of girls." And then, so he doesn't think my concern is just jealousy, I add, "I hope you were using protection."

"No matter how fucked up I am, I always do. I don't trust those girls. No one but you, Pep."

I don't know what he means by that.

I can hear the pleading in his voice, and I know that he needs me right now. He's right. He does need me. He's totally "rolling" right now with those dilated pupils, and he won't be able to fall asleep. He shouldn't be alone the rest of the night and I don't know what he'll do on his own anyway. What if he tried to drive somewhere? That would be bad.

"Okay, you can come over to my house." I pull out of the Wilders' driveway and park the car on the street outside our apartment.

Gran is asleep, but she's left my bedroom light on. I usually sleep in my underwear but I leave my sweatpants on when I crawl into bed. Jace slides in next to me. He shuts off the bedside lamp. "Can I take my pants off?" He asks. "I'll sweat my balls off if I don't."

I sigh. "Fine."

He takes his shirt off as well.

"You have underwear on, right?" I ask. This wouldn't be so awkward if we hadn't made out. We could pretend that we weren't attracted to each other.

"Yeah." Jace plops his head on the pillow. I lie on my side and watch him. He's on his back, staring at the ceiling.

"How do you feel?" I ask him.

"I don't know. That's a complicated question. I'm happy to be here right now. Really fucking happy to be with you."

"Let me guess. Ecstatic? That's why it's called ecstasy, Jace."

His eyes dart to mine and he rolls on his side to face me. "How do you know?"

"Gimme a break, Jace." I roll my eyes.

"Are you disappointed in me?" He asks in a low voice.

"Yeah, of course I am. But let's not have this conversation right now."

I can see his eyes in the darkness searching my face. "I won't do it anymore. If you don't want. If it means I can be with you."

"You won't do what? And be with me how?" My heart leaps in my chest. What is he talking about?

"I won't do drugs. I've been doing them. And be with you. Like this. Just like this. I could lie here every night and I'd be the happiest person in the world."

I know this is not the time to have this conversation. Especially because the sober Jace would never say these things to me. "Maybe we should go to sleep," I tell him.

"Can I hold you? Please? I won't do anything. I promise."

I snuggle closer and Jace pulls me into his chest, hard. He squeezes me to him and tucks his chin on top my head, tugging me as close as possible. After a few minutes he loosens one of his hands to rub my back, but keeps the other arm tight around my waist. I try not to think about what he was doing with other girls earlier that night. I know he needs me right now. Needs to know we're okay. *As friends.*

Or not . . . I can feel him pressed against my thigh, and there aren't a lot of layers between us. It makes me want to do things I really shouldn't want, and definitely shouldn't do.

"I know you can feel me," he says. "I'm sorry. I can't help it. But I swear I don't want to do anything with you. Well, I want to, but I want this more. I just want to hold you, okay? Ignore my dick."

"I can't ignore it, Jace." My face is pressed into his chest and my voice is muffled.

Jace adjusts himself so I'm still at his side, but can't feel him anymore. "Is that okay?"

I nod. This was a bad idea. But it's almost midnight, nearly two hours later than I usually go to sleep, and I'm exhausted. Jace strokes my hair and my back at the same time, and it soothes me to sleep.

★ ★ ★

When I wake up the next morning, I'm tucked into Jace's side like a football, and his throwing arm is wrapped around me. He nuzzles my neck like a cat. "Are you awake?" I ask.

"Yeah, but don't move. I like you here." His voice is scratchy.

"You should go home to get ready for school." Even though I'm quite comfortable, I know this shouldn't be happening.

"Five more minutes." He inhales.

"Are you smelling me?" I ask him.

"Yeah. You smell like the ocean or something. I missed it."

"I've never even been to the ocean," I remind him.

"What kind of shampoo do you use?" He pulls me closer to him.

"Jace!" I squeal and jump away from him when I feel him hard against my bottom. I must have taken my sweats off some time in the middle of the night because we're both in our underwear. "Is it always like that! Jeez!"

Jace chuckles. "It's called a morning wood. Sorry." But he doesn't seem the least bit sorry. He glances down at it. "He's waking up. Stretching, if you will."

I sit and cross my legs. "Ryan's picking me up in 30 minutes. And Gran's going to freak when she sees you. We need to get up." Jace sighs and rolls over onto his back, his erection proudly pushing up from black boxer briefs. He catches me staring and grins.

"Are they all like that?" I ask him. I should let it go, but m
fascination gets the better of me.

"Like what?" He knows what I mean, but he wants me to say it.

"That . . . big!" I cover my face with hands, mortified. It jus
seems so huge, and I don't understand how it can fit inside anyone
Jace pries my fingers away from my eyes.

"Don't be embarrassed. No, they aren't all the same size. Yo
must know that, at least."

I nod. Duh. "But do you know where yours is, like, size-wise?"

He raises his eyebrows. "What do you think?"

It's big. He knows it. Of course. He has all the other goods, wh
wouldn't he have that as well? I push him hard, trying to roll hir
off the bed but he doesn't budge.

He starts laughing and I smile. It's good to have Jace back. Th
cocky, care free, Jace. Maybe it will all be okay after all.

There's a loud knock on my door. "Jace Vernon Wilder! I knov
you're in there!" Gran screams. It's not a scream I recognize. Is sh
mad? It's hard to know with Gran. Jace and I look at each othe
with quizzical expressions.

"Coming!" Jace yells back. He pulls on his jeans and quickl
answers the door. Gran eyes his shirtless chest before moving he
gaze to me. I'm sitting in bed. At least the covers are hiding my bar
legs.

"Would one of ya like to tell me what is goin' on here?" She ask
calmly. Too calmly.

"It's not what it looks like, Gran," I tell her. "You know I went t
Wes's last night? Well, then we met up with Jace and he jus

decided to sleep here." I try to be as honest as possible. Not that drugs and orgies would necessarily shock Gran, but still.

"Hmph," Gran growls out.

"I assure you, Buns, there were no shenanigans." Jace sounds contrite.

Gran crosses her arms and looks back and forth between us. The mis-matching pajama set and piglet slippers diminish the impact of her piercing gaze, but only slightly. Apparently she's satisfied by her assessment because she turns to go back to the kitchen.

As soon as Jace looks back at me we break into another fit of giggles. It's like we're little kids again, and we know we're up to no good. Jace's six pack clenches as he laughs, and the temperature in the room increases. I clutch my stomach and roll back onto the bed to avoid thinking thoughts that I shouldn't.

"Okay, get outta here. I need to get dressed," I shoo him away.

Jace throws on his tee shirt and leans against the door frame. "So, does this mean you're not shutting me out anymore?" He asks.

I stare at the ceiling, avoiding his gaze. Does Jace need me? Do I have bargaining power? "Will you stop doing drugs?"

Jace takes a moment to answer. "Yeah. Okay."

Sheesh. That was easy. I push my luck. "Will you stop dealing drugs?" I say it quietly, just in case Gran is eavesdropping.

"Yes."

Definitely too easy. All I had to do was ask? I have a hard time believing him.

"You should go. Ryan's picking me up soon and I need to get ready."

"Can I start picking you up again? And dinner?" I glance at him standing in the door. He looks young and lost again, like he did last night. I so rarely see him like that, and it's impossible to resist.

"Yeah." I heave out a loud sigh, and I'm rewarded with Jace's heart-stopping smile. Just shoot me.

I hear Gran lecturing Jace while I pull on a pair of dark skinny jeans and a knit sweater.

"Young man, I don't know what you're up to but it's messin' with my granddaughter so you better clean up your act. You know I'm here for you, but you gotta wisen' up. Getting into a little trouble is healthy and you always were a bit of a trouble maker. But now I'm thinking you've been getting into some bad trouble. So get your shit together Jace Wilder."

"Yes, ma'am," Jace says. "I know what you're sayin'."

"Good."

They say a few more things to each other that I can't hear before the front door closes. A few minutes later, I'm brushing my teeth when I hear Ryan chatting with Gran in the kitchen. I haven't fully recovered from Jace being here. Ryan's newfound familiarity in our kitchen, so close to when Jace was here, is unnerving.

Gran hands me my lunch box and a cream cheese bagel for breakfast.

"I thought I saw Jace walking down the sidewalk when I pulled in," Ryan says when we're in his car.

"Oh, yeah. He was at our house." Shoot. I know this isn't going to sound good. "It's a long story." I take a bite of bagel to give myself a second to gather my thoughts.

"Oh?" Ryan prompts.

"Don't freak out, okay? Jace was kind of fucked up last night and I didn't want to leave him alone so he crashed at our house."

I peek at Ryan, and the hurt look on his face is like a kick in the gut. "I thought you guys weren't really talking right now?"

"We weren't. But I think I need to be there for him. Nothing happened between us though, okay?" Yet, I feel guilty.

Ryan pauses before he asks the question I know he doesn't want to ask, and I don't want to answer. "Where did he sleep?"

"We don't have a spare room, but we just slept."

"In your bed?" Ryan cringes, like it's painful for him to ask.

"Ryan, something is happening between us. With you and me, I mean." I quickly amend, knowing he could easily jump to the wrong conclusion. "And I hope it can keep happening, even though I know it was easier when Jace and I weren't speaking. But Jace is going to start being around again. Driving me to school, and dinner and stuff."

I don't want Ryan to give up on us yet. I've already formed a strong attachment to him and it scares me how much I hate the idea of Ryan moving on to Lisa, or someone else.

Ryan pulls into the senior parking lot. The radio is playing softly, and he sighs when he looks at me. His warm brown eyes harden with resolve. "Can I kiss you right now?" He asks.

I don't respond, but lean over the center console and gently brush my lips against his. He places his hands on either side of my face and softly kisses me back. He moves his head to the side, letting our lips slowly run along each other. His breath is warm against my skin. Ryan's thumbs skim back and forth along my cheekbones, and I sigh into him, letting my head drop to his shoulder.

"I'm going to be doing that a lot more, if that's okay with you," Ryan tells me.

"Permission granted."

Chapter 16

Even though the fainting episode is all over the Internet, none of my friends talk about it in the days leading up to Regionals. In fact, I think everyone must have decided not to get me worked up about qualifying for Nationals because my friends seem to avoid any mention of the race. I appreciate the sentiment, and surprisingly, it does help keep me from obsessing about the race.

After school each day, it's just me, Ryan and Coach Tom at practice. Charlie offered to help pace me at workouts, but I could tell he was enjoying his afternoons off with Zoe so I told him not to worry about it. Ryan and I are enjoying are the extra time together too. The transition from friends to more-than-friends is surprisingly easy. It's a natural development, and there aren't any complications, aside from Lisa giving me dirty looks in the hallways.

I can't help but contemplate what a transition to more-than-friends would be like with Jace. There's no question that it would come with a boatload of complications. Our different social circles being at the top of the list. Ryan's hybrid social status - as a runner and a popular senior - makes being together easy.

Ryan's parents invite me over for a pasta dinner the night before Regionals. I'm bringing a plate of meatballs out to the dining room table when Ryan's little brother, Kevin, joins me.

"So you're Ryan's girlfriend now, huh?" He asks.

"Sort of. How do you feel about that?" I don't know what else to say and it seems like he brought it up to give me his opinion anyway.

"It's cool. I like you way better than Katie. That was his girlfriend in California."

"Oh. Okay, well, that's good I guess." I'm not sure I want to know anything else about Katie. It's enough that Ryan was with her for almost three years.

"She was really mad they broke up," Kevin says in a loud whisper. "My room was next to Ry's and I could hear her sobbing and being all hysterical. It was funny."

"Kevin! That's not funny. That's sad. What if I cry and get hysterical if Ryan breaks up with me? I'd feel even worse knowing you would be laughing."

Kevin smirks. "It probably wouldn't be funny if it was you. She was just a drama queen so it was different." He shrugs. "Anyway, Ry would be an idiot if he broke up with you. But if he does, I'm happy to console you." Kevin grins widely and I laugh. He's pretty ballsy for a fourteen-year-old. I was under the impression he was shy, but I clearly pegged him wrong.

On the way back to my apartment later that night, I tell Ryan, "Your brother told me he'll console me if you ever break up with me. Looks like you've got some competition." I nudge him lightly in the ribs.

"And why would I break up with you?" Ryan asks.

I shrug. "He said your old girlfriend didn't take it well."

"Yeah, she really didn't," he says tiredly. "I think she thought we'd stay together when she went to college and then go on to get married."

"Does she still think that?" After all, it hasn't been so long since they broke up.

"I doubt it." But he doesn't sound so sure. "I'm sure she's met tons of guys in college."

I can't tell if I'm just being paranoid but I think I detect a note of regret in his voice.

* * *

The sky is filled with dark clouds when we arrive at the course the next morning. It's at a park south of Denver and I've never raced here before. I recognize a few of the girls from Colorado, but most of the people warming up are from other states. We are the farthest west state in the Midwest Region, and people flew in from places like Chicago, Cleveland, and Milwaukee. Some drove long distances from the Dakotas or Kansas. I almost feel guilty that Ryan and I got to sleep in our own beds and drove just one hour.

Not to mention the advantage we have from living at altitude. Denver is the mile high city, and people traveling from sea level won't be used to the oxygen deprivation.

I inhale the cool air, and think about the course I just walked through. It's incredibly hilly, and I like hills. The ominous clouds look like they'll break at any moment, and I love to run in the rain. Everything seems to be in my favor.

I adjust Jace's friendship bracelet that I tied onto my wrist last night. No point in being stubborn about it. I'll take any luck I can get.

The storm doesn't start gently. The boys race first and seconds after the gun goes off, a gust of wind blows across the course, bring with it sheets of rain. I jog over to Gran's car, and we huddle inside with the heat cranked up. I wish I could cheer for Ryan, but it's more important to stay dry and warm before my race.

"The course is going to be completely torn up for my race," I tell Gran.

"That'll be fun! You can get all muddy. Think of it like an obstacle course," she says excitedly.

"That's actually pretty good advice for someone who has never run a mile in her life." We exchange grins.

I huddle under a tree a few minutes before the race starts. Coach finds me and tells me to triple knot my shoes. "Once they get wet, they'll slide right off. I just saw a guy run by in nothing but his socks."

"Thanks, Coach."

"I'd give you a hug for luck Pep, but I'm drenched, and you're still pretty dry."

I wait under the tree until the last possible second to toe the line. It's a bit silly, since I'll get drenched immediately. My teammates drove down to cheer for us, and I'm glad they had the foresight to dress appropriately. I hardly recognize them all bundled up in rain gear when they approach me.

"Ryan won!" Omar exclaims.

I grin. No one says anything about what place I need to get (top ten, I'm all too aware) to qualify for Nationals so I can go to San Diego with Ryan. But they wish me luck.

"You love running in the rain, Pepper. Just do your thing!" Zoe encourages me.

"Have fun out there," Charlie tells me.

"I will," I say with a smile.

"Hurry up already or you'll miss the start!" Claire cries nervously.

I laugh and wave to my friends before heading to the starting line. Not surprisingly, I feel like I've jumped in a pool with my clothes on before the race has even begun.

Embrace it.

I'm nearly taken out right at the start line. When the gun goes off, I dig my spiked cross shoes into the mud, but find that it's hard to get a grip. There aren't as many girls in the race as Districts or State, but with all the slipping and sliding, I still have to keep my elbows out to prevent getting knocked over. We spread out after a few hundred yards, but I'm wary that I could find myself on the ground this time around for a completely different reason.

Just do your thing. I remember Zoe's words as I settle in with the lead group. Coach and I didn't really talk about a plan for this race, but I know what to do. Stay in the lead group as long as possible, and kick it up a notch at the end. We don't know exactly where I'll stand against the out of state girls, since I've never competed against them before.

The pace isn't too uncomfortable, but I can hardly make out the course in front of me, and I'm afraid I could trip at any minute. The mile markers aren't visible through the pounding rain, and the noisy wind prevents me from hearing anyone on the sidelines call out splits.

I'm guessing we're at about a mile when my foot lands in a deep puddle. I sink into mud up to my knee, and when I pull my foot out, I've lost a shoe.

The triple knots didn't work.

I don't even consider stopping to put it back on. Who knows if I could even fish it out of the mud puddle? It might be lost forever. There's no time to spare, and besides, I still have one shoe to help me maintain some traction.

The grassy part of the course that I walked through an hour ago is now like a slip n' slide. Charlie's voice bounces through my head. Have fun out there.

The rain soaks through my jersey so it clings to me like a second skin. I try not to let the sliding sock on my right foot mess with my balance as we wind down a hill. Leaning forward, the momentum helps me fly ahead of the pack with little effort.

Two girls won't let me take the lead, and when they pull in front of me at the bottom of the hill, I tuck in behind them. Their bodies protect me from the gusts of wind that threaten to knock us over. My ponytail whips around me head, and I focus on steadily moving forward and keeping my balance.

We've reached the last hill before the final stretch. I can just make out my teammates through the pounding rain. They are lined up along the steep incline, screaming my name.

At that moment, the sliding sock on my right foot catch on a root, or something on the ground. I pitch forward face first, with no time to brace myself. I swallow a mouthful of mud, and I'm sure I'm completely covered in it. I scramble up quickly.

The two girls have started up the hill, but I can still catch them. One is in a yellow uniform, and the other in red. The sock on my right foot has now come off, and I'm completely barefoot on my right foot. It's actually easier to grip the ground now.

Think of it like an obstacle course. Gran's full of good advice. She's probably freezing her butt off at the finish line, waiting for me to run by.

I dig my feet into the mud and embrace the burning in my quads. The harder I push, the deeper the pain in my legs and my lungs. But I'm closing the gap with the two girls in front of me, and that makes it worth it.

Just before reaching the top, the girl in the yellow uniform pitches forward and hits the ground. She's back on her feet already when I pass her, but she's lost her momentum. It's not easy to regain on this terrain.

I'm shoulder to shoulder with the girl in the red uniform when we hit the top of the climb. It's a straight 100 meters to the finish. I can barely make out the finish line through my mud caked lashes, but it doesn't matter. I'm not easing up.

I've got one shoe on, and I'm soaked in mud from head to toe. Literally. This is my kind of race. The discomfort from the elements is nothing compared to the throbbing in my muscles. I welcome it all as I force my legs into sprint mode.

The girl in the red uniform doesn't have a kick left in her and she disappears from my side as soon as I crank it up. I can just make out familiar voices screaming my name when I zoom in on the finish.

Cameras flash and I have to smile, because I just know those photos are going to be something else. I can already imagine a blown up photo of me covered in mud hanging over the fireplace. Gran will love it.

Chapter 17

There's not too much celebrating with my teammates immediately after the race. We're all ready to get home for hot showers and clean clothes.

I first rinse off all the mud from my body in a shower, and then soak in the bath. Jace calls to congratulate me, but we don't have much time to talk. He's at the State semi-final game and it's about to start.

After I blow dry my hair and change into yoga pants and a hoodie, the reality that I'm going to Nationals sinks in. It's a bit anti-climactic. I could tell that my friends and teammates expected me to qualify, even after the disaster at State. We have two weeks to fine tune before it's off to California, and a whole other set of competitive runners to confront.

My body is sore and tired, and I let myself doze on my bed. I don't normally take naps, but I did just win Regionals. I deserve one!

I *won* Regionals.

Regionals.

I beat the top runners from fourteen states.

Now what?

My phone ringing wakes me up some time later that afternoon. I see it's Wes on the caller ID.

"Hello?"

"Hey congrats! I heard you qualified for Nationals. I knew you would."

"Thanks."

"You know it's Jace's party tonight, right?" He asks.

That's right. Kayla and Andrea cornered me at my locker the other day at school and asked me to come. It was weird. I'd stopped going to Jace's birthday parties when he started high school.

"Yeah, I know about the party. His birthday is Monday," I say grumpily. Can't a girl get some peace and quiet?

"You going? I can give you a ride later."

"No, that's not really my thing, Wes. Are Lincoln people going?"

"Yeah. And CU. It's going to be huge. You should come."

"What's the point?" I ask. "I have Nationals in less than two weeks Wes, and a huge party isn't a good idea."

Wes sighs. "A couple of Jace's friends really want you to go. They said they asked you already, and they asked me to ask you because you told them no."

"Huh? Why do they even care?" I rub my eyes, and pat my bed for Dave to jump up.

"I don't know. They think Jace will be happier about the whole surprise party thing if you show. Not that it's even a surprise at this point," he adds.

"Wes, he's not going to care." In fact, I can almost guarantee he wouldn't want me there. "Seriously, I'm not going."

Wes doesn't push it. I'm already doing what I can, I don't need to change. I never went to his parties before.

Gran is at a knitting/smoking pot get-together, so I'm on my own for the night. Fortunately, Zoe calls shortly after I hang up with Wes to invite me over. She's inviting Charlie too, and I'm supposed to call Ryan.

"You can go to Jace's party if you'd rather, Ry. I know it's supposed to be this big thing," I tell him over the phone. We're technically together, but he still hangs out with Jace's group, and I don't want to be a party pooper.

"I would only go if you wanted to. I just want to hang out with you."

Awww, sheesh.

I decide not to change out of my yoga pants and hoodie. We're just going to lounge around anyway. All the holding back in training makes sense now. I am physically and mentally drained. Certainly not enough to keep me from feeling excited about Nationals, but I have to admit, Coach Tom knew what he was doing.

Gran has the car, so Ryan picks me up. He gives me a long kiss when I see him. Kissing each other hello or goodbye has become a regular thing over the past week.

"You clean up nice," Ryan tells me after taking in my yoga pants.

I raise an eyebrow. "I happen to think the mud covered look is quite sexy. On you, at least," I say with a wink. Flirty isn't usually my style, but sometimes Ryan brings it out in me. It's the dimples. He's so easy-going, it's hard not to simply relax and enjoy being with him.

"I'm so proud of you Pepper," Ryan pulls me in for a deeper kiss. The storm has stopped but it's still windy and cold outside. I burrow into his arms, and let the warmth from his kiss seep through me.

When we get to Zoe's place, it's a zoo as usual. Her parents ordered pizza, and her two little brothers and sister scramble around the kitchen counter when it arrives. When I spend time with the Burtons, it's easy to understand why Zoe is so chatty. Constant noise, every time I come over.

We head down to her basement after dinner to escape the chaos. "We've got tons of games, or we could play cards. Hey Pepper, what's the game called again that we play sometimes with your Gran and Lulu?"

"Oh, Euchre? Yeah that's a good game for four people. You guys know how to play?"

We teach Charlie and Ryan the rules, deciding on couple teams so that each team has one "experienced" player. At first, Zoe and I openly advise the guys about how to decide what cards to play, but the game quickly escalates to a fierce competition once everyone gets the hang of it.

"You guys want to finish this round and watch a movie or something? Or we have a hot tub if you want to go in?" Zoe asks.

"None of us brought bathing suits," Charlie points out.

"Hmm . . ." Zoe taps her index finger on her chin, mulling this over. "Pepper can borrow one of mine. You guys could borrow my dad's, or go in underwear?"

We decide to go with a movie, but it takes half an hour to decide on one. We end up going with *Up*, a cartoon with my favorite character ever, Doug, the golden retriever. Zoe and Charlie take one end of the couch, and Ryan and I squeeze into an oversized recliner together. I'm half on his lap, but he assures me he's comfortable.

When the movie ends, I see I have three missed calls from Jace. That's weird. I don't usually hear from him at night, especially on the weekends. There's one text.

u aren't here

I frown. Since when did I go to these things? I went to one party with Ryan, and that pool-cookout get-together at Wes's house, but that doesn't change the way things are.

I text back: *it's not my thing, u know that*

I hope he's being good and not doing anything stupid.

It's past my bedtime, but none of us wants the night to end. Ryan and I could go off to be alone, and let Zoe and Charlie do their thing, but I think there's some sort of tacit agreement that we're all better off hanging out as a group in this stage of our respective relationships. We decide to go in the hot tub, and apparently the guys are cool going in their underwear. My phone vibrates while I'm changing into one of Zoe's bathing suits. It's Jace.

"You're still up?" He asks.

"Yeah. What's going on?" I ask, concerned.

"Why didn't you answer earlier?" He sounds needy, and it's so unlike him that I'm immediately uneasy.

"We were watching a movie and my phone's on vibrate. Aren't you at your party?"

"I wanted you to be here. I told them that. They said they invited you. How come you didn't come?" His voice sounds funny, slower and faster all at once.

"Ummm... I don't know. I don't usually go to your birthday parties, Jace. I haven't since middle school."

He sighs heavily and I can hear loud music and voices in the background. "Can I come over?"

"And leave your party? Why? Aren't you having fun? How did the game go earlier?" Maybe they lost and he's upset.

"We won. But I just want to see you. Or you can come here."

"I'm at Zoe's," I tell him.

"Oh, that's not far from here right?" He asks.

"I don't know where you are," I remind him.

"Jesse's house."

"I don't know who Jesse is or where he, or she, lives," I explain to Jace.

Zoe comes back in the room with an armload of towels. She frowns. "Who's on the phone?"

"Jace," I tell her. She raises her eyebrows in question.

"Jace, just enjoy the party. We're celebrating your birthday with Gran on Monday, when it's your real birthday. Hang out with your friends."

People call his name in the background. "Okay. I just, I wish sometimes you were with me all the time, but I know it's better that you're not. I'm glad you're with Zoe." He sounds far away now.

"I know. Okay, I gotta go, we're getting in the hot tub. Have fun and be safe!" I know I sound like a mother, but really, that's all I want for him tonight.

I can't hear his response with all the background voices and he signs off a moment later.

"What was that all about?" Zoe asks.

"I'll tell you later." I don't know how to explain the conversation I just had because I don't understand it myself.

When we settle in the hot tub, Zoe looks at me and Ryan next to each other, with Ryan's arm stretched out behind my back. "So are you two, like, together now or what?"

I roll my eyes at her bluntness but glance at Ryan, who is smiling at me. "Whatever Pepper says."

I sigh dramatically. "I suppose you can call me your girlfriend if you want."

Ryan's smile widens. "So I'm your boyfriend now, huh?"

I shrug in response but lean in closer to him so he knows that I really mean it.

"Finally!" Zoe exclaims. "You're like, so perfect for each other. We all knew it was going to happen. Right, Charles?"

Charlie blushes. "Yeah, it's pretty classic. You guys are local celebrities and it seems right for you to be together."

Zoe bounces up and down in the hot tub. "Hey! Maybe they'll start calling you Pepyn. Or Ryper!"

We laugh at Zoe's enthusiasm. "If you try to make one of those names stick, I'm going to start calling you two Zolie or Choey," I warn her.

"I don't know, Zolie's actually pretty cool," Zoe says, laughing.

We hang out in the hot tub chatting until our skin starts to prune. The hot tub is outside and the cool night air feels good on my hot skin when I get out. I let myself air dry for a minute while the boys pull on the cover. They look pretty silly with their cotton boxer shorts clinging to their little runner butts. I try not to stare at Ryan, but I've never seen him like this and it's hard to look away.

"Pepper!" someone whispers loudly from the other side of the yard, where the fence door opens to the sidewalk. We look up to see two shapes walking toward us.

I recognize Jace immediately. His confident, smooth walk is slightly unbalanced. Remy is beside him. I can just make out their faces as they near us. Remy looks embarrassed and confused, but resigned. Jace is gazing straight at me but I refuse to make eye contact. I glance at Ryan, who's reaching for a towel to wrap around his waist.

"What are you guys doing here?" I ask quietly, but with unmistakable accusation in my tone.

"I'm sorry, Pepper." Remy puts up his hands, palms up. "He said he was coming here and I couldn't get him to drop it. I haven't had much to drink so I drove him. He's wasted."

Jace stumbles towards me for a hug and I can't do anything but hug him back. I see Zoe widen her eyes over Jace's shoulder.

"Hey, I thought you guys might want to come to the party," Jace says when he finally releases me.

"It's almost two in the morning, Jace. I told you I wasn't coming." I try to soften my voice, even though I'm frustrated. The air is filled with tension, and the expression, "you could cut it with a butter knife" comes to mind.

"But I'm your best friend. I thought I was at least." Jace looks around at the others, lingering a moment longer on Ryan. "And it's my birthday party."

"Can we talk about this later? This is Zoe's house. Her parents and brothers and sister are asleep. I don't think they'd be happy finding out more people came over."

We stand there for a moment longer, staring each other down. He wants me to go back to the party with him and I want him to leave. It's not a situation we've ever been in before. I can practically feel the power balance shifting in our relationship. The pieces that make Jace and me who we are, together, are all still there, but they are rapidly rearranging themselves. Finally, the dynamics between us settle into a new mold, and the tension in the air starts to lift.

"I'll go back to the party with you if you want," Ryan says to me.

Jace's head turns sharply to look at Ryan. Ryan looks like he wants to step back but he holds his ground.

I sigh. "Look, I'm exhausted. We just watched a movie and spent an hour in a hot tub. I was about to go home and go to sleep."

"I'll come," Jace says, and steps closer to me.

I don't know how to handle this Jace. He's still authoritative, and in control, even drunk. But he's being high maintenance. This side of Jace is still new to me, though it's becoming more familiar. And now, he's showing it to others too. He'll probably be mortified and furious when he sobers up. I don't want to deal with him then, that's for sure.

I want to tell him that he can't come home with me because Ryan's my boyfriend now, but I can't bring myself to cut into Jace like that when he looks so lost and exposed. I'd do it if we were alone, but not with others. I glance around at everyone, pleading for some sort of assistance with this situation.

Everyone is watching, waiting for my response. I don't mean to build the anticipation, but I feel like Jace and I are on a stage, and there's an audience. These types of exchanges between Jace and I are supposed to be private, and I'm incredibly uncomfortable. Instead of responding to his comment, I turn to head inside, grabbing a towel on the way. "I'm going in to change."

I'm grateful when no one follows me. I'm back in my yoga pants and hoodie when Zoe joins me in her bedroom. "What are you going to do?" Her voice is sympathetic.

"What do you think I should do?"

"I don't know. It's so awkward out there. I feel like Jace could crack at anything right now. You know how to handle him. But, Ryan's here, and things are so new with you guys. You don't want him to get the wrong impression." Zoe looks more concerned about my predicament than I am. I'm just frustrated, and terribly confused.

"I'm going out there." When I open the door, Ryan is resting on the couch armchair outside Zoe's bedroom in the basement. "Hey," I say softly.

"Hey," he says back. He has nothing but a towel around his waist. His hair is still wet, and there are droplets of water on his eyelashes.

I walk closer to him and he opens his legs so I can stand between them. "Jace isn't usually like this. I swear," I tell him. "I don't know what's gotten into him."

Ryan places his hands on my hips. "I do. He's afraid of losing you."

"But why? We went through a rough patch but things are back to normal again."

Ryan's warm eyes lift to look directly at me. "Are they?"

"Maybe not. There's you now."

The screen door opens and Jace walks inside. "Time to go home Pep. *Now*."

I glance at Ryan. "Go ahead," he says. "We're all calling it a night anyway."

Instead of kissing Ryan goodnight, I just give him a tired smile and squeeze his shoulders. Jace is standing in by the screen door glaring at me, and the last thing we need is him to cause a scene (more accurately, *another* scene).

Jace insists on sitting in the backseat with me on the drive home. He sits in the middle seat beside me and leans against my shoulder. I've never seen him drunk, and it's unnerving. How can I be so angry with him one minute, and so drawn to him the next?

"Slumber party?" he asks groggily when we pull up outside my apartment.

"Nope. Remy's taking you home." I push him off my shoulder and open the car door. The desire to take care of him is overwhelming. I could be a good friend and tuck him in, make sure he drinks some water and sleeps on his side. But friendship is dangerous when it comes to Jace Wilder.

"Goodnight Jace." It's my turn to draw the boundaries between us.

Chapter 18

I grip Ryan's hand when the plane starts down the runway, reviewing the safety information I've just read in my head.

He squeezes my hand and smiles at me. "How do you feel?"

"If this is it, I suppose I've had a good life."

"Oh, come on. It's no less safe than driving."

He puts his arm around me and I snuggle in to his chest, breathing in his smell that I've become familiar with. It's clean laundry and boy. I close my eyes, trying not to think about the rumbling feeling in my belly and the shaking plane.

Ryan rubs my back. Lying on Ryan's chest reminds me of the bus ride on the way to Districts when I fell asleep on his shoulder. I started to fall for Ryan that day, but the fall was gentle. Like his kisses. It wasn't a long fall either. I sense that he's holding back. Or maybe it's me. It's probably both of us.

"Are you excited to get back to California?" I ask him, once we've taken off and I'm no longer clutching his tee shirt with a death grip.

"Yeah, I am. I'm not planning on seeing many friends though. We'll get in today, tour the course, race Saturday, and then we head back Sunday."

"I bet you could have stayed a few more days. The teachers wouldn't have cared if you missed school."

"We're coming back for Christmas and staying through New Year's, so I'll see everyone then."

Nationals is only an hour from Ryan's home town, but we are all staying at a hotel. Ryan's uncle offered to host us but we thought it'd be easiest to be close to the course.

When we exit the terminal at San Diego International Airport, a girl our age runs up to Ryan and wraps her arms around him. She has beautiful wavy light brown hair, and long tan legs. When she disentangles herself, I recognize her from some of Ryan's Facebook photos. It's Katie. Two guys behind her greet Ryan with brief, less aggressive, hugs. Katie turns to Mark and gives him a hug as well.

"Hey guys. This is a surprise!" Mark says.

"We wanted to surprise Ry!" Katie beams. "Mikey came up from UCLA for the weekend, and you know Chad and I are at USD, so there's no way we're missing Ry's last high school meet!"

"Thanks, guys. You really didn't have to do that." Ryan says, but I can tell he's psyched to see his buddies. I'm too overwhelmed to understand my feelings at the moment. I would have thought Ryan would mention that his girlfriend of three years goes to college here.

"This is my Coach, Tom, and my girlfriend, Pepper." Three sets of eyes settle on me. I get the feeling the girlfriend thing is news to them.

"That's cool that you came all the way out here to support Ryan," Chad says.

Mikey punches Chad in the arm. "She came to race, dumbass! Haven't you followed this? These two are big news in the running world. Same high school, and they're both going to Nationals. Pepper Jones, right?" Mikey puts out his hand and I shake it.

Ryan and I get a ride to the hotel with his friends while Coach Tom and Mark pick up the rental car. I somehow end up in the middle between Ryan and Katie. Talk about awkward.

The guys chat away. Ryan tells them about Brockton, and they fill him in on college stuff. I can practically feel the coldness from Katie. Bubbly one minute, and icy the next. I guess it isn't the reunion she had in mind. I almost feel guilty, but I know I shouldn't.

"I'm going to take a shower and unpack. I'll let you guys catch up. Coach said to meet in the lobby around 2, right?" I ask Ryan. I have my own separate hotel room. Ryan's is down the hall.

"Yeah, but that's a couple hours from now. Come on over to my room when you're ready, or we can meet in the lobby."

"I think I'm just going to rest, but I'll come by if I change my mind."

The hotel room is the nicest I've ever stayed in. Actually, I've only stayed in a few others, all with teammates for cross or track meets. I have this one to myself. I call Gran to let her know I made it. Then I call Jace, but it goes straight to voicemail.

I slip on a hotel bathrobe and wrap my wet hair in a towel after showering. I lie on the bed and turn on the television, but I'm not really watching it. I have another hour to kill before we head over to check in and walk the course. I've never felt so lonely in my life.

***

Everyone seems to know Ryan when we walk the course. It takes twice as long as it should because a runner or a coach stops us every few minutes, all wanting to talk to Ryan. This is his domain. And he's the reigning champ.

Mark and Coach Tom each head off to meet up with friends in the area for dinner while Ryan and I grab dinner at the hotel's restaurant. It would be romantic, except that Ryan's friends join us. Katie takes the open seat next to Ryan and I end up directly across from her, between Chad and Mikey. Her chair is practically touching Ryan's. She glances often at me throughout dinner, making it hard to ignore her.

Chad and Mikey are cool, and they distract me from my anxiety about tomorrow and my annoyance with Katie by telling stories about college. Katie keeps trying to pull Ryan's attention away by speaking quietly to him so that no one else can hear. She touches him constantly, and Ryan seems perfectly comfortable with it. After all, she was his girlfriend for three years. That's a serious commitment. It must have been something really special. I shake my head and swallow the lump in my throat.

As soon as I'm done eating I toss some cash on the table to cover my meal and tip. "Hey guys, it was great to meet you all. I'm going to head up to rest for tomorrow."

Ryan glances up from his conversation with Katie. "You don't want to chill for a little while? It's only 7:30. We could all watch a movie or something in my room."

I make the mistake of glancing at Katie, who is glaring at me. "Nah, I'm exhausted. Goodnight, guys." I hesitate for a moment. I would normally give Ryan a hug, or maybe a peck on the cheek or something, but it doesn't feel right. Not with Katie sitting there clutching his arm, and his two friends who have only ever known him as Katie's boyfriend sitting there watching. Ugh. I give him a pretty pathetic attempt at a smile before heading towards the elevators.

I'm brushing my teeth in the bathroom thirty minutes later when I hear a knock at my door. I check the peephole before opening the door, aware that I am wearing only sleep shorts and a tank top. I see Ryan on the other side and I feel the tightness in my chest ease slightly.

I open the door and stand to the side so he can come in. "Hi," I say softly. "Are you guys going to watch a movie in your room?"

"No, I told them I should probably get to bed early." Ryan scratches the back of his head and sits down on the edge of my bed.

"Yeah." I lean against the dresser, unsure what to say or how to act. Though I hate sounding like a jealous girlfriend, there's no point in denying it. "So, um, it seems like Katie is still really into you. I'm not going to lie, Ry, it was a little weird for me seeing how close you guys are."

Ryan raises his eyes from the floor to meet mine. He sighs heavily. He stands up and places his hands on my hips. His eyes search mine. "I'm sorry, Pepper. I didn't want to be rude to her. I know she was a little more touchy than necessary, but I really don't have feelings for her anymore."

"I believe you. But that doesn't mean it didn't make me feel terrible." I speak softly. I'm not angry. I'm not sure what I am. I don't think he really has feelings for Katie anymore, but just the history of their relationship hurts me.

My phone buzzes, alerting me to an incoming text message.

"Do you want to check it?" Ryan raises his head to ask.

"Nah, I will in a minute."

Ryan takes my hand and leads me over to the bed. We lie down next to each other, and my heart rate picks up. I've never been on a bed with Ryan before.

"I've been wanting to do this all day," he says before bringing his mouth to mine. This kiss is passionate, more demanding than the soft ones we've shared in the past.

His hands roam along the side of my body, and his thumb brushes my breast. He continues caressing me past my waist and stops at my bottom. Underneath my pajama shorts.

My body instantly reacts, and I press closer to him. He deepens the kiss, and I let my own hands drift from his neck to his chest.

My cell beeps again, reminding me of the unchecked text.

"We should stop, Pepper," Ryan says shakily.

"We should?" I ask. The erection pressing into my thigh does not agree.

"It won't take much for me to lose control with you, Pepper. And that's the last thing I want. Especially tonight."

"You're probably right." I know he is, but my body is on fire, and it's incredibly difficult not to give in to the desire when he's lying here right next to me.

When our ragged breathing slows, Ryan sits up and hands me my phone from the nightstand. It's from Jace.

Call me to say goodnight.

I glance at Ryan, wondering if he saw the message when he picked up my phone. If Katie had sent Ryan a message like that, I would not have liked it one bit. But then again, I didn't date Jace for three years. He's just my friend. Except, not really. Ugh.

Ryan's watching me. I throw my phone on the bed and take his hands, leading him to the door. "I'll see you at breakfast at 7:00?" I ask.

Ryan nods before reaching up to cup my cheek. "You're really amazing, Pepper, you know?" He shakes his head and kisses me softly on the lips. It looks like he wants to say more, but instead he just says, "Sleep well."

"You too." I tell him, closing and locking the door behind him. I lean back, taking a deep breath.

When I call Jace, he answers on the first ring. "Hi Pep!" He says enthusiastically.

"Hi, Jace." Loud music blares in the background. No surprise there.

"How's California? Did the flight go okay?" He asks.

"It's great. Yeah, the flight was good," I tell him.

"What's up? You sound kind of down. You miss me, don't you?" I can hear him breathing, like he's walking upstairs. The background noise fades.

"Of course I miss you. I'm not down though. Maybe a little lonely in this big hotel room, but mostly just nervous for tomorrow."

"You're gonna be amazing," he says earnestly. "Just run like you always do. You've got a gift, Pep."

"Thanks, Jace."

"I wish I was there," Jace says.

"In San Diego? You'd like it here. Didn't USD recruit you?" I ask him.

"Yeah, but I meant there, with you, in your hotel. So you aren't lonely."

"Jace," I warn. It wouldn't have been weird for him to say that several months ago. He's always wanted to take care of me. But now . . "It wouldn't be right for you to be in my hotel room," I murmur.

I can practically see Jace's jaw clenching when he says, "You better be sleeping alone tonight."

"Relax. Ryan and his dad are sharing a room. Besides, I need to get a good night's sleep." I smack myself if the forehead, realizing exactly what I've implied with that statement. That Ryan and I wouldn't be sleeping. "I just meant, I'll sleep better in a room by myself, you know?"

"You've slept fine with me in the past," Jace points out. I notice he smugness in his voice. It's true. Aside from the night he slept in my bed recently, we used to share a bed all the time during sleepovers growing up.

"I should get to bed, Jace." I don't like the direction this conversation is going.

"Okay. Smile, baby." He pauses, presumably waiting for me to smile. I do. "I'll be thinking of you when you're running tomorrow."

When I lie in bed, trying to fall asleep, I find myself longing for Jace to be there, holding me.

* * *

I sit with some of the other girls on the midwest Regional team at breakfast the next morning.

"You are so lucky to be on the same team as Ryan Harding," one girl tells me. "He's so hot."

The other girls at the table watch Ryan, who is talking to his dad across the room. "He's super nice too," another adds dreamily.

"I think he has a girlfriend. Or he did last year. She was following him around the whole time before and after his race," another girl, who apparently raced at Nationals last year, says with a bit of disdain.

The girls glance at me, waiting for confirmation. "Oh, um, yeah I met her. Katie. She's his ex-girlfriend now."

"Oh, he's coming over!" someone says excitedly.

I glance up and Ryan smiles at me. He says hi to everyone at the table and then crouches down next to me. "Morning," he says softly.

"Morning." I smile, remembering his sweet goodnight kiss.

"How'd you sleep?" he asks.

"Took me awhile to fall asleep, but it was okay."

"Same." He glances at the girls at our table, apparently deciding we don't have enough privacy to continue the conversation.

"I'm going to sit with some guys over there," he nods towards a table with guys from our regional team. "Let me know when you're ready to head out." He kisses me on the cheek before heading to the breakfast table.

When I glance up, the expressions on the girls' faces remind me of the day that Jace kissed my head in the school cafeteria. I shrug. "We're together."

The girls groan, embarrassed by their earlier comments. "Then you're even luckier than I thought!"

I smile proudly. "Yeah, he's a really good guy."

I try to ignore the way they blatantly check him out. Ryan really does have a great body, especially for those of us who appreciate distance running.

Gran calls me to wish me luck during breakfast, and I'm surprised to get another text message from Jace this early on Saturday morning telling me he knows I'll be awesome. I feel guilty that it makes me feel so warm and fuzzy to know how much he cares.

Ryan takes my hand when we walk through the lobby towards the rental car. "All the girls were talking about you at breakfast this morning before they realized I was your girlfriend," I tease him. "I better watch out, you've got a lot of admirers."

Ryan laughs. "Pepper, if I told you what guys think of you. . . it's me who needs to watch out, believe me." He shakes his head, amused.

My phone beeps every several minutes on the way to the course with good luck messages from everyone on the team. Ryan's is buzzing as well and we laugh when we realize we're getting the same texts. I'm surprised when I get one from Wesley though.

"Why is everyone up so early on a Saturday morning anyway?" I ask Ryan.

"There's going to be a live streaming video online, you know that, right?"

"What? Really! Dang, I should have had Jace set it up for Gran so she could watch. Bummer."

"I'm sure if you called to ask him, he'd do it." I don't doubt Jace would head right over to our place, but I need to focus on the race right now, and not worry about who's watching it.

When we get to the park where the race is held, my stomach is in knots. I've never raced this course. My teammates aren't here. Gran's not here. Ryan puts an arm around my shoulder.

"Hey, don't look so worried. You're going to do great."

Easy for him to say. He's done this before. On this same course. And it's practically his hometown.

I'm trying to ease my nerves enough to get my number pinned to my singlet without stabbing myself when I hear a familiar voice say, "Can I help you with that?"

I look up at mischievous green eyes. I can't contain the squeal that comes out of my mouth. "Jace!" I jump into his arms, wrapping my arms and legs around him like a monkey. He stumbles back.

"Whoa, Pepper! I'm happy to see you too." His voice is muffled in my hair as he hugs me back.

It's not like it's been a long time since I've seen him. Less than a day. It's just that he's here, in San Diego, to watch me run at Nationals! With Jace's football and baseball schedules, he rarely gets to see me race.

He puts me down. "What are you doing here!?" I exclaim.

He raises an eyebrow. "I'm here for you, of course."

"You flew all the way here to watch me race?"

"I did. Technically, I'm on an official recruiting trip to USD, so they paid for the flight."

"Oh." It would stink if he went to USD. Too far away.

"But between you and me," Jace leans down to speak in my ear. "I'm going to sign for CU."

I slap him on the arm. "That's not very nice, Jace. Taking advantage of recruiting trips."

He shrugs. "They don't care."

"So how did you get here from USD?"

"A friend from football camp is at USD and he let me borrow his car."

I feel an arm around me and glance up at Ryan. I realize how close I am to Jace and I step back.

"Hey, man. This is a surprise, huh?" Ryan asks. He hasn't shown much jealousy up to his point but his voice is unnaturally tight.

"Yeah, I couldn't miss it."

"Oh! I dropped the pins when you got here, let me find them." I avoid the awkward moment and get down on my knees to look for the safety pins I dropped in the grass.

"Here, let me help you out." Jace takes them from me and holds the bottom of my singlet as he pins it up for me. His movements force Ryan to take a step back, dropping his arm from me.

"Ryan, hi!" Katie bounces up to him and wraps him in her arms. Jace glances up at her for a moment and then back at me.

"Ex-girlfriend," I tell him.

Jace doesn't say anything while he continues to adjust my number, and I'm really thankful he doesn't check her out. Ryan glances as me while Katie fawns over him. When we make eye contact, the irony of the situation dawns on me. What is happening here?

I blink and break eye contact with Ryan. Now is not the time to think of it. I feel a twinge of guilt that Jace's presence will mess with Ryan's focus, but it immediately disappears when I realize his ex-girlfriend's surprise visit does the same thing to me.

"I've gotta warm up, Jace," I tell him when he finishes pinning the number to my jersey.

"Go do your thing. I'll be here." He gives me another hug.

"Warm up with me?" I ask Ryan.

"Sure."

As we head off, I hear Katie introducing herself to Jace. He's here for me, but Jace won't turn down an opportunity to flirt with a hot girl. I just hope that's all he does.

★ ★ ★

Coach told me that some girls might take off at a crazy pace and try to break away from the get go. He was right. Two girls sprint ahead like it's a one mile race instead of 3.1. I know the girls at this race are supposedly the fastest in the nation, but there's no way they'll maintain that pace.

I settle in with the main pack. The pace is definitely faster than I'm used to. I can see Jace out of the corner of my eye, and it gives me confidence that I belong in this race. Earlier today, my main goal was not to embarrass myself. Now, I want to kick ass. I want Jace to be proud of me. I want to make it worth his trip to watch this.

We catch and pass the two girls who broke away by mile two. Coach told me that if I felt good at this point, I should go for it. But this pace is quick, and I don't think I can pick it up. Listening to the labored breathing of the four other girls still running in the lead with me, I know I'm not the only one hurting.

A tall girl in the lead group wearing a Northeast Regional singlet starts to push the pace, and I sense the other girls dropping off. I recognize her from the photo in *Running Fast Magazine*. It's Jessica Lillis, the girl who got second last year and is expected to win. I follow her lead when she pulls ahead, even though my lungs and legs are already screaming. I've never raced this hard. There's still half a mile to go and I already feel the same way I typically feel in the last one hundred meters.

I can hear Coach yelling something at me from the sidelines, but everything around me is a blur. All I can see is Jessica's braid swinging in front of me as she sets the pace. There's screaming and noises all around me but I can't process it.

Until I hear Jace's voice. It's brief, only for a second, as I pass by where he's standing. "Stay with her, Pep! You got this!"

I repeat it in my head like a mantra. Stay with her. Stay with her. Stay with her.

My legs hurt. My chest hurts. I want to ease up, not press harder. Second place would be awesome. I'd be happy with second place. Thrilled, actually. That's what my body is telling me. It wants me to drop back.

Then I hear Ryan's voice. "Take her, Pepper! Pass her!" I can do this.

I move to the side to look ahead. I think I can see the finish line. It's probably four hundred meters away. That's only one lap around the track. It's nothing. I can do this.

Pass her. Pass her. Pass her. I chant in my head. But I'm pushing as hard as I can and I'm right next to her. Stride for stride. She's not slowing down. Isn't she tired? Why can't she slow down?

Then I see Jace. Right next to the finish line. How did he get there so fast? He's yelling but I can't hear him. There are too many other people yelling. I can see him though, and the expression on his face urges me forward. He really wants me to win. He wants me to beat this girl. I dig deep. Deeper than I ever have before.

My vision blurs and I start to see dots dancing in front of me but I keep pushing, digging, pressing forward. I don't even know if Jessica's in front of me, beside me, or behind me anymore. When I feel my body pass through a ribbon, I know I've reached the finish. I blink several times, and try not to collapse. No need to be dramatic here. I can stay on my feet. I look around.

Jessica is next to me. I don't know which of us won, but I know I should hug her to congratulate her for a good race. I must be delirious. Why am I hugging a sweaty stranger?

I stumble away from the finish line, a volunteer pointing me in the right direction to get past the barriers. "Congratulations!" I hear over and over. People are patting me on the back.

I snap out of it when I see Jace with a huge grin on his face. He wraps me in a hug. "Holy shit, Pepper! That was incredible!" He lifts me off the ground and swings me around. "You're the national champion!"

So I *did* win!

★★★

The feeling of euphoria doesn't fade when Katie smothers Ryan after he wins the boys' race. It doesn't fade when Jace has to head back to USD later that afternoon. Euphoria lasts through the night, on the plane ride home, and when our teammates meet us at the airport. And maybe it is the feeling of euphoria that helps me face the truth. It's not until I'm lying in bed late on Sunday night that I make the decision to break up with Ryan.

And as soon as I make the decision, I know I can't dwell on it. I need to talk to him. I send him a quick text message.

You still up?

Can't sleep. What's up?

Can I come pick you up?

Ryan calls me. "Is everything okay?" He asks.

"Yes, of course. Sorry. I can't sleep either. I want to see you." I almost say, I want to talk to you, but I don't want to get a break-up conversation started over the phone.

"Ok. I can come to you, if you'd rather."

"Nah, I feel like driving anyway. I'll be there in a few minutes."

I pull up to his house ten minutes later, and he heads out the front door wearing sweatpants and a parka like me.

He looks hot with his disheveled hair and concerned expression. I want to kiss him. Good thing I decided to do this now, when I was sure of it. I know it's the right thing to do.

We drive to a park near his house. It's a cold night, but I don't want to sit in the car. "Swing set?" I ask him.

We sit on the swings next to each other. I've never had a boyfriend so I've never broken up with anyone. I figure, in this instance at least, honesty is a good way to go.

"Ryan, I think we should end things between us." I look at his face for a reaction, and he doesn't seem hugely surprised. Phew.

"After the race, Jace was hugging me, and Katie was hugging you, and the moment made me realize this might not be our time. Things are good between us but, well, I guess I haven't let my feelings for Jace go, like I thought. And I'm sorry for that."

He's watching me with those ocean blue eyes. He doesn't look angry, or sad. Maybe a little hurt, but mostly just thoughtful. I wish he wasn't so good looking. It's distracting. Moments pass. "Say something," I whisper.

He shakes his head. "I know I should probably just accept what you're saying, but I need to try to talk you out of it."

That definitely wasn't what I was expecting. He was happy to be patient and wait it out before.

"If this is about Katie, I want you to know that I never felt about her the way I feel about you. It was easy to be with her at first, and then it never made sense to break up. I can't even compare you two, really." He rocks back and forth on the swing and looks up at the sky.

"She took me by surprise this weekend. I thought she'd be over me, and move on at college. I haven't spoken with her much since I moved here." He turns in the swing to look at me. His explanation doesn't change anything, but I let him continue, sensing he needs to get this off his chest. "I would have told her to back off if I knew how much it was bothering you. I just didn't want to be an asshole to her."

"It's okay, Ryan. I get it." And I do. "But I still think this isn't our time to be together. I think you might feel that too."

He looks up at the stars. "Maybe. But you're not an easy girl to let go."

Chapter 19

"Gran, I think the newspaper clippings posted all over the house are getting a little excessive," I tell her Tuesday at dinner.

"Shush. Let a grandmother be proud of her little hot shot granddaughter." She waves her fork in my direction in disapproval.

I roll my eyes. "It's just weird seeing pictures of myself everywhere in here. I can't look anywhere without seeing an article." She's posted clippings on the cupboards, the fridge, and the walls throughout the hallways.

"I didn't put any in your room," she points out.

The front door opens and Jace walks in. "How's the Brockton High Phenomenon doin'?" He gives me a hug from behind.

"I thought you weren't getting in until later tonight?" I ask

"Came straight here. I missed my favorite girls."

"Lemme grab ya a plate." Gran heads to the kitchen before Jace can protest.

"So you saw that article in the Post yesterday already?" I ask. It was on the front page, with photos of Ryan and me breaking through the finish tapes, and titled "Brockton High Phenomena." I suppose it's pretty cool that two people from the same high school won Nationals, but the press coverage is starting to get embarrassing.

"Yup. I haven't missed any of the news this weekend." He sits down across from me with a giant grin and winks. Oh. So he knows about Ryan and me. I spoke to Jace on the phone last night and hadn't mentioned it. But I'm not surprised someone told him. Apparently all of my business is Jace's business.

Gran returns with a plate and silverware. I'm thankful she's here, because I don't know what's going to happen with Jace and me. I've thought of a million scenarios, but for all I know, nothing will change. Maybe Jace already has plans to hook up with some other girl tonight. It really wouldn't surprise me.

After dinner, Jace asks, "Wanna come over to start that Hendrix puzzle we got ages ago?" He asks.

I glance at Gran. "Did you finish your homework?" She asks.

"Yeah." I didn't, but I really want to hang out with Jace.

When we get to Jace's house, I settle in on the den sofa by the puzzle table. Before I can get too comfortable, Jace takes my arm and brings me into his bedroom.

Pulling me flush against him, he crushes his lips to mine. I push my hands through his hair, letting the sensations of tongue and lips heat my body. The ferocity and determination of his kiss tells me he's been waiting to do this for a while. Maybe as long as I have.

The moment breaks when we hear the sound of pounding feet coming down the stairs.

"Who's that?" I ask. Jace said that Jim was at his girlfriend's house.

Jace frowns. "I don't know. Stay here." He heads to the den, and I stay standing in the middle of his room, unsure what to do.

"Wolfe, Rex, what's goin' on?" Jace asks. "Since when did you come over here unannounced?"

"We called man, but you're phone was off," Wolfe says.

"You've been out of town all weekend, and Wes said you'd be back today," Rex says.

"So? You know I'm out, man. I don't have anything for you. You can't come by here like this anymore, got it?" Jace is angry, no doubt about it. I can just imagine his jaw clenching and his fists flexing.

"Nah, we know man, but we gotta talk to you. Wes is out now too, and what are we supposed to do? You guys won't tell us your supplier. How are we gonna get what we need to distribute? We got clients countin' on us man," Wolfe pleads.

"Your supplier's gonna need to unload to someone else, Jace. Why don't you give him our names?" Rex asks.

"Look guys, when I said I was out, I meant it. My supplier knows about you guys, but he didn't sound like he was planning on reaching out to you. It's not my business. Got it?"

Rex and Wolfe grumble in response. A few minutes later, I hear footsteps going up the stairs.

Jace returns to the room and shuts the door. He rubs his face. "Those two are fucking idiots."

"I'm glad you're done with that, Jace."

"Hope it's really done. What Rex and Wolfe haven't figured out is that my supplier was a gang member. Gangs are real choosey about who they deal with. I think they're gonna use their own gang members to distribute at CU now," Jace explains.

"Why didn't they do that before?" I ask.

"Good question. They're based in Denver. Don't really have a lot of guys in Brockton I guess." Jace looks lost in thought. "But it doesn't matter anymore. Where were we?"

"I believe you were standing there." I point to a spot in front of me and tug him closer to me. "And I was standing here." I take a step forward so we're only inches apart.

"And what were we doing?" Jace asks with a smirk.

"Let me show you."

I hope you enjoyed my debut novel! Pepped Up is the first in a series that follows Pepper Jones through high school and into college.

Find me online at:

www.alideanfiction.com

www.facebook.com/alideanfiction

www.twitter.com/alideanfiction

www.goodreads.com/author/show/7237069.Ali_Dean

CPSIA information can be obtained
at www.ICGtesting.com
Printed in the USA
FSHW021320110520
70129FS